Christmas
IN HIS ARMS

AVERY CHANDLER

The characters and events portrayed in this book are fictitious. Any similarity to persons, living or dead, is coincidental and not intended by the author.

Published by Avery Chandler
www.averychandler.com

ISBN: 978-1-7350848-1-7

Cover by Frauke Spanuth/Croco Designs
Interior formatting by Author E.M.S.

Published in the United States of America.

To those who feel as if they have no voice, who have lost themselves: You matter. You deserve a better life. Find your courage and take the first step toward freedom. Visit thehotline.org and seek the help you need.

CHAPTER ONE

The snow struck her in the face while blinding flakes bit into her skin. It was nearly midnight, and Sarah Walsh trudged through the New York City streets in search of a hotel room. She gripped the edges of her jacket, wishing she'd brought a hat or gloves. But there had been no time.

The throbbing pain of her bruised cheek kept her going. *I'm not going back to him. I can't.*

After two years of marriage, she couldn't live in the shadow of fear any longer. Her husband had struck her cheek with his fist, sneering, "If you want to leave, then go. You're an idiot if you think you can get anywhere without me."

Ben didn't believe she would do it. He probably thought she'd come crawling back, broken and subservient. Not this time. She couldn't.

Her hands were trembling, though it was from more than the cold. It was the bone-deep fear within her that he was right. She had no job, no family in the city, no friends at all—Ben had made sure she stayed isolated.

All she had left were the clothes on her back, one credit card, and forty dollars cash in her pocket.

She touched her hand to her aching cheek and tried to push back the fear. *Keep walking. Keep moving forward. Find a hotel. You can figure the rest out later.*

The warm glow of the Harrow Suites illuminated the snow only a block away. She wasn't sure she could afford the hotel, but maybe the rate would be cheaper this late at night. Then again, every room in the city cost hundreds of dollars per night. But she had a credit card, and that was all she needed right now.

Sarah trudged past piles of snow and black trash bags lined along the curb. She heard the familiar sounds of sirens and taxis blaring their horns while men and women crossed the busy streets. Scaffolding set up against a building offered a temporary shelter as she walked past the delicious aroma of a 24-hour coffee shop. What she wouldn't give for a hot, steaming mug right now. Her torment continued when she passed a bakery with glass cases displaying freshly baked muffins and pastries. She'd skipped both lunch and dinner today, and her stomach reminded her that missing the meals had been a very bad idea.

When she reached the revolving glass doors of Harrow Suites, Sarah stepped into the lobby and took a moment to warm herself. She didn't know how bad the swollen mark on her face was, but she might be able to pass it off as rosy cheeks from the cold.

Her hands were still shaking, but she felt better with each step forward. *It's going to be all right,* she told herself as she approached the front desk. *You'll be safe now.*

A woman in a navy blazer with blond hair in a French twist smiled at her with a silent invitation to approach the front desk.

Sarah hesitated, rubbing her hands together to ease the numbness. Another man was leaning against the doorway to the office. He was reading a piece of paper, his expression frowning. His dark brown hair was the color of polished wood, and he wore a charcoal gray suit tailored to his broad shoulders and lean waist. She guessed he was in his mid-thirties, and his face held the look of a man who carried a great deal of responsibility. A manager, she was certain.

When he spared her a fleeting glance, her nerves tightened. He was easily one of the most attractive men she'd ever seen—but then, two years of marriage had taught her that appearances were deceiving. Handsome men held a power of their own, an ability to get whatever they wanted—and that was the last thing she needed in her life right now. Instinctively, she shielded her thoughts, shoving back the raw emotions into an invisible box.

"Can I help you?" the front desk clerk asked. "Do you have a reservation?" Her gaze lingered a moment on Sarah's face, but her smile remained.

"No, but I was hoping you'd have a room available." *As cheap as possible*, she thought to herself. She didn't know how long it would take to find a job or if anyone would hire her.

The clerk's expression turned sympathetic. "I'm so sorry, but we're completely sold out. There's a convention in town, and we don't have any rooms left." She added, "If I knew of another hotel that had a room,

I would call them for you. But as far as I know, everything is full."

"I'm sorry to hear it." Sarah managed a nod, as if it were nothing. But inwardly, she felt the rise of tears threatening. She couldn't imagine returning to the streets at this hour in search of a hotel room.

She walked away from the desk but couldn't quite bring herself to go outside. At least, not yet. The blizzard was raging, and she didn't want to leave the warmth of the building.

Sarah walked over to one of the lobby chairs and sank into it. Her gut clenched, and she closed her eyes, trying to think of what to do now.

She'd been so stupid to leave her cell phone behind, but at the time, she was afraid Ben would find a way to track her with it. Now, she wished she had it so she could call other hotels. Instead, she'd have to use the phone at the front desk if they would let her.

Tears burned at her eyes, but she bit her lip hard. *You can't fall apart right now. Keep going.*

"Excuse me," a male voice interrupted. Sarah looked up and saw the manager from the front desk. His gaze fixed upon hers, and he frowned at the sight of her swollen cheek. His eyes were icy blue, and he had a faint dark bristle of beard on his cheeks, as if he'd been too busy to shave.

Her heart pounded at the sight of him, and she tensed. "Yes?" For a moment, she half-expected him to ask her to leave. The lobby was for guests, not for people who had no place to stay. And heaven knew, she looked homeless right about now. Her hair was soaked from the snow and so was her jacket.

4

Instead, the manager spoke quietly. "If you still need a room, there is one available." His tone held a hint of compassion, and tears blurred her eyes. "Cora didn't know we had a last-minute cancellation."

Relief flooded through her, and Sarah tried to gather her thoughts. She closed her eyes, pushing back the fear. It was going to be all right—at least for tonight. "I'm so glad," she murmured. With a pained smile, she added, "I really didn't want to go back into that storm."

"I would have called a cab for you," he said.

She was glad he hadn't. Right now, she needed to save every penny she had left, and a cab was a luxury she couldn't afford.

"Just check in with Cora, and she'll set you up." Though his demeanor was only professional, she sensed his sympathy. Her throat closed up, and she warned herself, *Don't cry.* Instead, she stood and murmured her thanks again, trying to brave a smile she didn't feel as she approached the front desk.

Sarah gave her credit card to the front desk agent, while she filled out a registration card. After she handed it back, there was a moment's pause.

"I'm sorry, but your credit card was declined," Cora said. "Do you have another method of payment you could use?"

Oh God. She didn't have to ask why the card was rejected. Ben must have called and cancelled it.

For a moment, it felt as if her entire world had spun out of control and back into his circle of command. Panic gripped her stomach, and she felt the shame rising up. "I'm sorry. I don't have another card," she mumbled. And there wasn't enough cash to cover the room.

Numbly, she stepped back, wondering what to do now. She returned to the lobby chair, and every step reminded her that she'd failed.

Outside, the storm pounded flakes against the glass windows. She needed a few moments to gather her courage. She could try to go to a shelter, but in this weather, it would be hard to find a place. Not to mention, Ben might find her there. She was convinced that he would hire people to look for her.

Hot tears gathered again, but she squeezed her wrists hard to hold back the emotions. She refused to cry. Tears wouldn't do anything to solve her problems.

In her peripheral vision, she saw the manager watching over her. She couldn't stay here much longer. She wasn't a guest and had no right to stay in the lobby. Slowly, she took a deep breath and collected her courage. She didn't have any money for another hotel, but she might be able to slip into the stairwell and hide for the night. It was so late, no one would look for her there. If not here, then in another hotel. And first thing in the morning, she would start looking for a job.

With the decision made, she stood from her chair and turned around...only to find that the manager was standing in front of her.

"I was just leaving," she started to say, but he cut her off.

"No. You're staying here tonight."

Alec Harrow hadn't missed the swollen bruise on the woman's face or the shame in her eyes. He knew all the signs of abuse. When her credit card had been declined, she'd looked beaten down, as if another fist had plowed into her jaw. Someone had hurt her, and she needed sanctuary. He wasn't going to let her go out into the blizzard tonight. If that meant giving up his own suite for the night, so be it. He could always return to his apartment if he decided to set aside the night's work.

As the owner of Harrow Suites, he had forty hotels to manage along the east coast and another hundred hotels in Europe. One room was reserved for him in every hotel, and he made a habit of dropping in without notifying the staff. It was the best way to ensure that the hotels were running smoothly, and he prided himself on the chain he had built.

Alec studied the young woman discreetly for a moment. She was slender with shoulder length honey blond hair and a heart-shaped face. Her green eyes held such pain, he wondered how any man could try to hurt a woman. A large diamond rested on her left hand, and he suspected her husband had caused the blow. She wore jeans and an oversized sweatshirt that hid her figure. Her jacket was unzipped, but it was only a windbreaker—not nearly enough to push back the cold wintry air.

But more than that, he saw the stubborn pride in her face as she stood up to face him. "I'll be all right."

The woman was going to walk out of the hotel and into a blizzard, wearing that pitiful excuse for a coat. He could tell that she'd left with the clothes on her back and hardly anything to call her own. She wouldn't accept his help, and if he didn't stop her, she would leave. He couldn't tell her that he was giving up his own room for her use, so instead, he thought up a lie.

"It was a mistake. The credit card went through the second time when I told Cora to try it again. It must have been a system malfunction."

The look of relief on her face was stunning. "Really?" She closed her eyes a moment, and then smiled. "I'm so glad."

He didn't return the smile. Seeing her circumstances only brought back all the memories he'd tried to bury over the years. He had a thousand unanswered questions about this woman, but he knew better than to ask.

Don't get involved, he warned himself. *It's not your battle to fight.* He knew that, and yet, he couldn't stand by and let this woman go out in a blizzard on a night like this.

He escorted her back to the front desk and said, "Cora will get you the key cards, but you'll need to wait until the room is made up. I'll call Housekeeping." Jasmine lived down the street, and he could offer her overtime pay to come in and clean the room.

Alec excused himself to make the call while the woman signed the registration card. He stood at the doorway with the phone in his hand, though he hadn't even dialed the number. Eavesdropping was much easier that way.

Cora put two plastic keycards in an envelope and said, "I'll hold on to these for now until your room is ready. If you have a cell phone number, I'll text you when the room is ready."

"I don't…have my phone with me," the woman said. "I'll just wait in the lobby if that's all right."

"Of course," Cora said brightly. "There's coffee at the station over there. Help yourself."

Alec watched as the young woman walked back to

the lobby chair. The pieces were starting to come together. She had no cell phone. One credit card that had been cancelled. Likely very little cash, and he didn't know if she'd eaten a meal tonight. After she left the desk, he made the call to Jasmine and then a second call to room service for a tray of food.

"Mr. Harrow?" Cora asked in a low voice. "Are you sure about this?"

"That bruise didn't come from a fall," he muttered. "And yes. It's only for one night." He hadn't planned on sleeping much anyway. This property wasn't making enough of a profit, and he needed to spend time with the accounts and unravel where the problems were. He could work in the office for a few hours and return home once it was finished.

Cora had a worried look on her face, but she nodded. "You're a good man, Mr. Harrow."

"Don't tell anyone." The business world wasn't kind to the softhearted. He'd built Harrow Suites from a small boutique hotel in the city, taking endless risks until he'd created a worldwide hotel chain. It was a fragile empire, but when it came to expansion, most of his rivals knew better than to underestimate him.

With that, Alec closed the office door, trying not to think of the woman in the lobby. He brought up a few of the spreadsheets he'd been working on, but he couldn't concentrate. The numbers blurred together, and after half an hour, he gave up. A knock sounded at the door, and when he called out, "Come in," he saw that the room service tray had arrived. He'd been careful to choose an assortment of appetizers, cookies, and soft drinks instead of a full meal.

"Thank you." He signed for the charge and added a generous tip before he picked up the tray and walked into the lobby.

The woman was sitting in a large chair with her knees tucked beneath her while she stared out at the falling snow. It took her a moment before she noticed him standing there with the tray.

"You missed our complimentary appetizer hour," he said. "We usually offer our guests drinks and snacks in the evening. I thought you might be hungry."

She glanced at the tray as if she wanted to refuse, but her eyes lingered on a brownie. Her mouth pursed as if she were trying to keep from reacting to the food. When she hesitated, he asked, "Would you rather have a soft drink or coffee?"

The mention of a hot drink brought a warmth to her eyes. "Coffee would be great." She drew her knees down and stared at the tray.

"Cream and sugar?"

She nodded but didn't speak. Alec walked toward the coffee station but caught a glimpse of her reaching for the brownie. She ate the entire thing in two bites, and the hard knot in his gut drew tighter. Then she reached for a cookie, making him wonder how long it had been since she'd eaten.

He poured the coffee and brought over a second cup filled with flavored creamer cups and sweetener packets. She stopped eating the cookie and her face turned sheepish. "My grandma always said to start with dessert first. That way you always have room."

Alec passed her the coffee and she held it a moment, warming her hands. Then she added four creamer pods and three packets of sugar. For a moment, she reminded him of a little girl, doctoring up her coffee.

"Do you want a cookie before I eat them all?" she offered. With a wry smile, she said, "I probably will."

Alec shook his head. "I've already eaten." He hadn't, really, but he wasn't about to take her cookies. Not when she was clearly so hungry. "I'll leave you to them."

"Thank you, Mr...?" She let the question trail away, but he wasn't about to give his last name. Not when she could connect his identity to the hotel chain.

"You can call me Alec. And it was my pleasure."

"I'm Sarah." She didn't offer her last name, and he didn't ask. It was better for them to remain strangers.

He intended to leave but couldn't quite bring himself to go. At least, not yet. "Is there anything else you need?"

"Not unless a job is something else you have on that tray," she remarked before she shook her head. "I'm just kidding. Thank you for your help. I really do appreciate it." This time, her mouth curved in a genuine smile. It lit up her face with a softness and beauty that caught him off guard. Though her blond hair was still wet from the snow and a tangled mess, he found her fascinating.

He turned away and saw Cora raising her hand to catch his attention. Then she pointed toward Sarah and held up the key card packet.

"Your room is ready," he told her. "You can finish eating first if you like. Or take the tray with you." Though he already knew the answer, he asked, "Do you have any luggage you need brought up to the room?"

She shook her head. "No, I don't have anything." His gaze fixed on the bruise on her face, and she blushed at his stare.

He understood her need to keep that boundary intact. "I'll send up some of our complimentary toiletries. Enjoy your stay."

Her room was at the end of a long hallway. When Sarah put the keycard inside the slot and opened the door, she was startled to realize that Alec had given her the largest suite in the hotel. The lights were already on, and the carpet had just been vacuumed. The room smelled clean, and it had a large living room and a desk that faced a floor-to-ceiling glass window overlooking the city. A king-sized bed stood at the opposite end of the room, and there was a small bar with a silver tray and an ice bucket upon it.

There was a familiar scent within the room, like a man's aftershave. It took her a moment to realize what it was. Or, in this case, *who* it was.

Alec had given her his own room. She couldn't say just how she knew, but she was sure of it. Though it was foolish, she returned to the door and deadbolted it before flipping the latch over. He didn't seem like the sort of man to lure an unsuspecting woman into his room, but she was taking no chances.

Outside, the snow raged against the windows, piling up on the street. Lines of cars were stopped in traffic, despite the late hour. Sarah picked up a blanket from the edge of the bed and wrapped herself inside it. She felt the familiar rise of anxiety as she wondered what she would do tomorrow. Somehow, she had to find work. But a fast-food job wouldn't pay enough for a hotel room.

She had a degree in interior design that she'd never used. But what good was that? It would take time to earn the money she needed. No, the higher priority was finding a place to stay that was within her budget. A hotel wasn't a good solution, since Ben could cancel the credit card at any time—not to mention, he might not pay the bill.

A twist of nausea caught her stomach, and she gripped the edges of the blanket, feeling lost. But instead of pitying herself, she tried to look at the positive moments of the day. She had a warm bed to sleep in, and Alec had brought her food.

Just thinking of him brought a flush of embarrassment. It had been so long since a man had been kind to her instead of ordering her around. Ben had controlled every moment of her day, from the time she woke up, to what she wore, to the way she lived her life. Everything had revolved around him.

She'd been so stupid to fall for her husband's romantic gestures. At the time, she had been flattered by the two dozen roses or the gold watch he'd given her after only one month of dating. What woman didn't want to fall in love with a rich man who seemed to adore her?

She had married him only six months after she'd met him, star-struck by the man who had showered her with affection. But Ben didn't know the meaning of love. Once she'd moved in with him, the imprisonment had begun.

"You won't need to get a job, Sarah," he'd said. "I've already cancelled your interviews."

She'd been shocked that he would do such a thing,

but his eyes had softened. "I'm going to take care of you. I make enough money, so you don't have to work. I've arranged for everything you need."

He'd opened the closet to reveal dozens of designer labels, matching shoes, and handbags. All were arranged by color, the garment hangers facing the same direction. At the time, she'd been thrilled by the gift, believing that he was the most generous husband. But it was only the beginning.

"Your stylist has made a list of what you are to wear each day. You will be expected to look your best at all times, especially when we entertain guests at home. You will never leave without your make-up on or your hair done." He stepped back, his face somber. "I know you aren't accustomed to attending formal events, and that isn't something I expect or want from you. In fact, I want to keep our marriage a low profile. I value my privacy, and I want to protect you. The media isn't kind."

It was as if he'd wanted to hide her from the world. Sarah had argued that she was perfectly happy to attend parties with him, only to realize that he had no intention of taking her out in public. He had been grooming her for the role of a subservient wife who stayed at home to meet his every need.

Ben had donated all her old clothing, but she'd managed to save one sweatshirt and one pair of jeans. When she'd worn the sweatshirt on her escape to this hotel, it had felt like she was holding on to a precious memory, as if her mother were watching over her. The sweatshirt was one that Rosalie had owned, years ago. It was the last memory Sarah had of her before her mother had died of cancer.

She didn't even realize she was crying until the phone rang, interrupting her thoughts. It was late, nearly one-thirty, and she wondered if it was the front desk or Alec. When she picked up the phone, she answered, "Hello?"

"I'm glad you found a place to stay, Sarah."

Bile rose up in her throat, and the blood seemed to freeze in her veins. She nearly hung up on her husband, but managed to ask, "H-how did you find me, Ben?"

"The credit card charge. It wasn't difficult." His voice had that smug quality that she loathed. "I asked them to notify me of the first charge after I froze the account. I'm surprised you had enough cash to cover the room."

She said nothing, trying to gather command of her emotions. So, her suspicions had been right. This was Alec's room, and he'd allowed her to stay, free of charge.

"I will send a car to pick you up in the morning," he said. "And you will not attempt to run away again."

This time, she did hang up. And when the phone rang a moment later, she let it go to voice mail. The last thing she wanted was to hear her husband's commands. Instead, Sarah went into the bathroom to run the shower. She turned on the hot water and rested her hands against the sink as the mirror fogged up.

Anger and frustration raged within her. Ben expected her to return to the prison she'd endured within their marriage—after he punished her, that is. She could only imagine what he would do to her for running away.

When she wiped the humidity from the mirror, she studied her swollen cheek, which was already starting to bruise. He would only hurt her again if she went back.

15

Next time, he might break her ribs or worse. She couldn't do it. Not again.

You're going to be strong now. You have to be.

Alec rubbed at his eyes and took a sip of coffee, exhaustion weighing on him. He'd spent most of the night going over a contract proposal. If this deal went through, Harrow Suites would be the exclusive hotel chain for all business travel with Venture Enterprises. He had a meeting with the CEO later this week to work out the details.

A soft knock interrupted his thoughts, and he looked up to see Cora standing at the threshold. "I've finished with my shift, Mr. Harrow. But before I go, I thought you should know that Ms. Walsh is in line to check out from the hotel."

He blinked a moment at the mention of the name. Was she talking about Sarah? He hadn't actually heard her last name before now. "Thank you, Cora."

A voice inside warned him not to get involved. He had given up his own room last night to a woman he didn't know, and if he stayed inside the office, she would walk away, and he'd never see her again. It was better that way.

And yet, when he saw Sarah hesitate at the desk, staring at the blanket of snowfall upon the ground, he was torn between wanting to help her and knowing he shouldn't. The last time he had tried to help a battered woman, he'd been too late. At the very least, he wanted to ensure that Sarah was safe.

Before he could stop himself, he started to walk towards her. She paused a moment and looked back at him. Her eyes held an emotion so intense, he hardly knew whether it was fear or uncertainty.

"Do you have a place to go?" he asked quietly.

She froze and glanced outside before shaking her head. "Not yet. But I'll find something."

"Do you want me to call a cab for you?"

Her expression turned wary. "No. I can walk."

He could already guess her thoughts—she didn't have the money for a cab. "I'll pay the driver to take you anywhere in the city."

She stiffened and shook her head. "That's all right. I'll be fine."

But pride wasn't going to feed her or give her a roof over her head. If he let this woman walk out the door, he didn't like to think of the consequences.

"I wanted to thank you for giving up your room to me last night," she said softly. "It was kind of you."

He kept all emotion from his face as he nodded acknowledgement of her thanks. *Let her go,* his conscience advised. *This isn't your fight.*

But he'd walked away once before, and he'd regretted it every day of his life. Now, he had a chance to change that.

Before he could stop himself, Alec tossed common sense away and told her, "If you still need a job, I need someone to do temporary housekeeping during the holidays. You could stay here until you find full time employment."

Logically, it wasn't a good idea to hire a stranger. He knew nothing about this woman, aside from her name.

But then, it was only for a few days. Wasn't it better to provide her with a job and shelter? And they sometimes took on extra temporary help during busy seasons. One of the housekeepers could train Sarah.

She still hadn't answered, and he added, "Dawson Green is one of my managers. Tell him I sent you, and he'll arrange for you to get a uniform and training for the job."

He turned away, as if it meant nothing at all. But he saw her falter, twisting the diamond ring on her left hand. His uneasy gut feeling heightened.

"I would like that," she said. "But I'm afraid my husband will find me here. He said he was sending a car for me today."

"Who is your husband?"

"Ben Carnell," she answered. There was a flash of fear on her face, but she squared her shoulders. "He knows I was here last night."

Alec kept his face neutral, but inwardly, he knew what a mistake it was to get involved. This situation was delicate because Ben Carnell was the CEO he had a meeting with later this week. If they reached an agreement, it would mean millions of dollars in profit over the next few years. But if the deal didn't go through, he might have to close at least three hotels, including this one. He would do everything in his power to avoid laying people off after the holidays.

Alec could only imagine what Carnell would say if he knew what had happened last night. It grated over his conscience that he had to make a deal with the devil. He'd gone over the numbers, and without the contract, there was no way to save the hotels.

He debated what to do, turning the problem over in his mind. At this time of year, all the shelters were full. And someone like Sarah Walsh would never survive. She was a billionaire's wife who knew nothing about how to live on the streets or how to survive on minimum wage. She wouldn't last an hour.

She wasn't his responsibility—not like the employees were. But if he gave Carnell's wife a job and a place to stay, he was risking a multimillion dollar contract. He was risking *their* lives and the lives of their children. Was one woman's safety worth the livelihood of so many others?

He already knew the answer. Just as he knew it was easiest to let her make her own decisions.

"Stay or go," he said at last. "It's your choice."

CHAPTER TWO

Sarah knew he wanted her to leave. It was written all over his face, in the tension of his shoulders. The offer was only temporary, and so was the room. Her pride was screaming at her to say no. But what other choices did she have? He was giving her not only a job, but also a warm place to sleep at night.

While she thought it over, she asked, "Aren't all of your rooms booked? Because of the convention?"

He swung back and stared at her. "Some of the guests are checking out. Or you can stay in the housekeeping storage room if you want. There are rollaway beds."

That made more sense, and she nodded. "I would be grateful for a few days more. But please don't tell anyone I'm here. If Ben calls, let him believe that I checked out." It would buy her a little more time, until she figured out where to go next.

"Was he the one who hit you?"

Sarah didn't want to admit the truth, but there was no point in trying to deny it. "It was my fault for making Ben angry. I should have kept my mouth shut." She pushed back the memory, reminding herself that it was over now. Even so, it was harder to push back the fear. A part of her wished that he hadn't hit her. She could have forgiven him for angry words. She could have blotted them out, choosing to remember the good moments in their marriage instead. It hurt to realize that there was no turning back—he wasn't the man she'd thought he was.

Her heart ached with denial. She had never in her wildest dreams imagined that the handsome, charming man she'd married would become someone else. But when they were alone, the mask had come off, and Ben had started reshaping her into the wife he thought he deserved. She'd tried so hard to please him, telling herself that his demands were only meant to help her fit into his life.

Now, she no longer knew who she was. A shell of a woman, erased by a man who wanted her to become someone else. It took every last bit of strength left within her to face Alec and admit she needed help.

When she met his gaze, she saw bridled fury in it. "It wasn't your fault. No man should ever hit a woman. There's no excuse."

She couldn't answer him. Although a part of her knew he was right, he didn't understand that she had lived with Ben's behavior for so long, she was used to it.

"I know," she said, because it was the expected answer. But it was hard to believe it.

In the past, after Ben had yelled at her, he would apologize and bring her flowers, promising never to do it again. *"It's just that you're better than this,"* he would say to her. *"I look at you and see how beautiful you are.*

How perfect. I don't want you to ever be less than you should be."

She had been a possession to him, not a person. When they'd married in secret, he hadn't wanted her to take his last name. At the time, she hadn't protested, for what did it matter? Now, she wondered if he'd wanted to distance himself from her.

The thought of going home made her stomach twist with nausea. Sarah took a hesitant step backwards and then said, "Where should I wait for Mr. Green? I can't stay here in the lobby or Ben might find me."

"You can wait in the office behind the desk," Alec suggested. "If you keep the door closed, no one will see you. But even if he does know that you're here, you don't have to leave with him. I have my own security."

His offer made Sarah feel slightly better. She was starting to think that Alec was the general manager of the hotel. He had the air of superiority, as if everything was within his command. But it wasn't threatening—instead, it made her feel protected.

"Thank you," she said. Her nerves were still twisting within her, but at least she had a place to stay for another night or two. The promise of a job gave her the chance to earn a little money. Even the smallest amount would help.

She was grateful that breakfast was included for all guests, and she'd eaten as much as she could this morning. That way, she could ignore lunch and wait until dinner tonight to save even more money.

Alec opened the door to the office behind the front desk, and Sarah went inside. She chose a seat across from the desk but decided to leave the door slightly cracked. It made it possible to stay out of view but still see who was arriving.

A moment later, a well-dressed man carrying a briefcase strode behind the front desk. His black hair was shaved close, and his skin was a rich brown. "Mr. Harrow," the man greeted Alec, shaking his hand. "It's always a pleasure to have you visit our property."

Harrow? No wonder Alec hadn't given his last name. Alec Harrow wasn't the general manager of the hotel—he was the billionaire owner of Harrow Suites. His hotels spanned the east coast, and he also owned properties overseas.

Oh God. She'd escaped one wealthy powerful man, only to run into another one. Her gut clenched, though she knew the fear was irrational. Alec had done nothing at all except offer her a safe haven. But she wasn't used to men being nice without wanting something in return. She gripped her hands together, trying to center herself and push back the fear.

"Dawson." Alec greeted the man with a handshake. "It's good to see you."

"How long will you be staying with us, Mr. Harrow?" Although the words were spoken with a pleasant tone, Sarah understood that it was a subtle way of inquiring why Alec had come.

"Another day or two," he answered. At that, Alec closed the door and lowered his voice, making it impossible for her to eavesdrop on their conversation.

She stayed hidden for the next few minutes, awaiting her fate. Her heart was pounding, and even the scent of fresh coffee made her stomach churn. She hated not being in command of her life. Sitting in an office, waiting on other men to make decisions about a job or shelter, made her feel utterly helpless. And she loathed that feeling. She promised herself that once she earned a little money, she would find a way to support herself.

The door to the office opened, and both men approached her. Sarah gripped her hands together, not knowing what to expect.

"Ms. Walsh, this is Dawson Green, general manager of the hotel."

Sarah wished she were wearing more appropriate clothes than the raggedy sweatshirt and jeans, but she managed a nod. "Hello."

"I was telling Ms. Walsh that she could stay here for a few days and fill in for any of our housekeepers who want time off."

Mr. Green smiled warmly. "We would be glad of the extra help. I've called Jasmine and she'll bring you a housekeeping uniform to wear."

She didn't know what else Alec had said to him, but there was no trace of pity or annoyance on the general manager's face. He didn't ask why she needed a place to stay, nor did his gaze linger on the bruise upon her cheek. The kindly smile on his face threatened to break apart her fragile emotions. "Thank you."

Alec held out his hand. "It was a pleasure meeting you, Ms. Walsh. I wish you well." She shook his hand, and he held it for a moment before releasing her fingers. The warmth lingered upon her palm, and she pushed back the wellspring of emotion. She had learned her lesson about getting involved with wealthy, powerful men, even if his actions were only meant in sympathy.

Though Alec's tone was formal, completely devoid

of any personal involvement, there was still no denying that he had given up his room for her. His actions went above and beyond charity. He had given her a way of keeping her pride, and even if that meant scrubbing toilets, she would do whatever was necessary.

Mr. Green guided her away from the front desk and toward the housekeeping staff room. Before he opened it, he stopped. "I wouldn't share anything about your living arrangements with other staff members," he said. "Mr. Harrow arranged for a complimentary room as a courtesy, but he's never done that for any other employee. Keep it to yourself."

She nodded and promised she would. Then the manager opened the door and introduced her to a woman named Jasmine. Jasmine was in her mid-thirties with a sturdy build and a riot of black and red curls crammed into a bun. She eyed Sarah as if she didn't think she'd ever cleaned a room in her life.

"This is Sarah," Mr. Green told Jasmine. "I want you to find a uniform for her and train her. She'll be helping out, doing some temp work." He added, "If you or Maria want some time off for the holidays, make sure Sarah knows what she's doing first."

The wary expression on Jasmine's face didn't change, but she nodded. "Yes, sir."

As soon as he'd gone, Jasmine eyed her. "You ever cleaned rooms before?"

Sarah met her gaze evenly. "I cleaned my apartment every day before I was married. Just show me what to do, and I'll do it."

Jasmine glanced at her cheek. "Did your husband give you that?"

She nodded. There was no point in trying to pretend otherwise. "It's why I'm here. I left him."

At that, the woman's eyes softened with sympathy. "Been there myself." With a sigh, she said, "Let's get you a uniform."

Alec already knew this was a bad idea, letting her stay. One wrong move, and everything would unravel. But when she'd said it was *her* fault that Carnell had struck her, it was like hearing the echoes of his past. He'd tried not to interfere the last time, but his mother Eva had paid the price. There was no neutral ground in this. He couldn't stand back, no matter how hard he wanted to stay out of Sarah Walsh's private battle. All he could do was offer her the means of fighting back.

When he'd given her a job this morning, hope had blazed in her eyes, and it had softened a dormant part of his heart. It was impossible to ignore his instincts to rescue a woman in trouble. But he was treading on the edge of something else, a greater threat to his business, if he didn't close himself off.

A black sedan pulled up to the curb and his instincts went on alert. He immediately recognized Ben Carnell striding across the salted sidewalk. He wore a woolen overcoat, leather gloves, and a tweed flat cap. A flare of anger caught Alec when he saw the man walk inside, but he masked it. There was a look of self-importance on Carnell's face as he approached the front desk.

Alec remained in his office with the door cracked. Jasmine should have taken Sarah up to the third floor.

There was no reason they should return to the lobby, but even so, he remained wary.

Dawson greeted the man at the front desk, and Alec overheard him say, "I'm so sorry, Mr. Carnell, but your wife left a few hours ago. We called her a cab."

"And where, exactly, did she go?" Carnell kept his voice pleasant, but there was an undertone of fury beneath it.

"I have no idea. I'm sorry." Dawson waited for him to leave, but Carnell didn't move.

Instead he said, "I want to speak with your general manager."

"I *am* the general manager," Dawson replied. "Is there something else I can help you with?"

The annoyance deepened on Carnell's face, though he kept a thin smile. "I want to talk with Harrow. He should be here since we have a meeting this week."

"I will see if he's available," Dawson answered. He knocked upon the door, though it was still cracked open.

"Come in." As soon as Dawson opened the door, Alec added, "Close the door behind you."

His general manager obeyed, and Alec said in a low voice, "I want you to page Housekeeping and make sure Sarah doesn't come downstairs under any circumstances." He met Dawson's gaze, and understanding passed between them. This was a fragile situation, one that could erupt in his face and threaten his hotel chain if he didn't handle it properly.

He stood from the desk and opened the door, striding toward the front desk. He faced Carnell and greeted him. "Hello, Ben. I thought our meeting was scheduled for Friday. But if you'd like, I can arrange for us to have coffee in the restaurant, and we can discuss our business now."

"I'm not here about the hotel contract," Carnell said in a clipped tone. "My wife went missing, and she checked into this hotel last night."

He had to be careful in the way he chose his words. "Did she? I wasn't aware."

Dawson met his gaze in a silent alliance. "I was telling Mr. Carnell that she checked out of the hotel hours ago. She took a cab and left."

"I want to see your security footage," Carnell insisted. He had a look of rage on his face, as if someone had stolen his prized possession, like a dog had run away, instead of a wife.

Alec's resolve tightened, though he kept his expression impassive. He wasn't about to endanger Sarah by revealing her whereabouts.

"It may be best to let the police handle a domestic dispute," he said. "I'd be happy to call them on your behalf."

The irritation only heightened on Carnell's face. "No. Not yet. But if she returns…"

"I'll call," Alec said. Though he had no intention of doing so whatsoever. He looked the man in the eye and said, "I'll see you on Friday at our meeting."

Carnell straightened and met his gaze. "Until Friday."

There was something mind-numbing about cleaning. After ten hours of scrubbing bathtubs, vacuuming, and dusting, Sarah was exhausted and ready to drop. She had scrounged up lunch by taking an apple from the breakfast lounge, but her stomach was roaring for food now. Jasmine had already clocked out, and Sarah sat down for a moment, trying to decide what to do. All her money was in their joint bank account, and she had no means of touching it. She cursed herself that she'd left her ATM card and driver's license behind. Fear was a powerful motivation for leaving, but it had left her reeling, unable to think clearly. With no phone, no money, and no identification, she had cornered herself. If only she could send someone to get them, it would help.

The phone rang, and she answered. "Housekeeping, may I help you?"

"This is Dawson Green. Is this Sarah?"

"Yes, it is." The familiar twist of fear caught in her stomach. She had finished her work for the day, but now she wondered if there was a problem.

"Mr. Harrow has asked to meet with you. Could you come down to the front desk, please?"

"I'll be right there."

But the familiar nerves gathered within her, snowballing into the fear of being forced to leave. She knew she couldn't stay here for very long. It wasn't possible. And yet, her terror of the unknown stretched out before her. Although Mr. Green had warned her not to come downstairs when Ben had arrived, she couldn't hide indefinitely. She had no doubt that her husband *would* find her. What then?

She took the elevator downstairs and caught a glimpse of her reflection in the mirror behind her. Jasmine had given her the gray housekeeping uniform, and the outfit sagged on her, though Sarah had cinched the waist with the white sash.

The elevator doors opened, and she glanced around before she approached the front desk. Mr. Green was waiting for her, and he held a manila envelope in one hand. "Mr. Harrow asked me to give you this. Then he wants to meet with you in Barnaby's at 7:00."

Barnaby's was the hotel's upscale restaurant. Why would he want to meet with her there? She was about to ask, but her stomach reminded her that the meeting would likely involve free food. And that wasn't something to be ignored. Given the choice between a meal and vending machine snacks, it was really the only option. She took the envelope, uncertain of what it was.

She went to sit down in the lobby lounge, choosing the chair farthest away from the front door. When she opened the manila envelope, she saw a room key card, a hundred dollars in cash, and a note.

Enclosed is your salary for today's work, along with a room where you can stay. I saw your husband this morning. We need to talk.

Her heart froze at the news, though she should have been expecting this. No doubt Alec—no, she should call him Mr. Harrow—would ask her to leave soon. This couldn't go on for very long...but then, she refused to think of that now. She could only handle one day at a time. And for tonight, a hot shower would feel amazing after the day's work. Over a hundred guests had checked out of the hotel, so there were plenty of spare rooms now that the convention was over.

She was torn between her desire to see the room and wondering what he wanted from her. Her suspicions darkened, but she returned to the elevator and pressed the button for the fourth floor. It wasn't the same room she'd stayed in the night before, and she didn't know what to expect.

When she walked down the hallway, she found room 412 and inserted the key card into the lock. It opened, and she entered the darkened room with a king-sized bed. She flipped on the light switch and saw a large square box on the bed. Was that supposed to be there? Or had they accidentally given her the wrong room?

She found a tag with her name on the box, so that answered her question. Inside the box was a pair of black trousers and a peacock blue silk long-sleeved blouse, along with a pair of black leather heels. There was also a gift card to Chatham's department store on Fifth Avenue with a phone number to call for a delivery of any necessary undergarments.

A tightness clutched her gut from deep inside, and it reminded her of all the clothes Ben had chosen for her. There were endless rules about what to wear and when. If she dared to choose something the stylist hadn't already selected, her husband had sent her upstairs like a wayward teenager. When she had asked why she couldn't attend parties or galas with him, the answer was always the same—*I want to keep you all to myself and enjoy our privacy. If the media finds out about our marriage, you'll never have any freedom again.*

But those two years of marriage had been little more than a prison. She'd felt like a doll, dressed up and put away in the house, waiting for someone to take her out.

Anger gathered within her, and she shoved the box off the bed, feeling the rise of hot tears. No. She would not wear the clothes selected for her. She would not become another man's puppet.

Her stomach growled again, but she pushed back the hunger. Right now, she wanted a hot shower, and then she would confront Alec Harrow. Though maybe he believed he was helping her by giving her clothes, she could never accept such a gift.

Alec was surprised when Sarah arrived at Barnaby's wearing the housekeeping uniform. He stood up from the table and gestured for her to sit, but there was no mistaking the tension in her expression.

"Thank you for joining me," he said.

She did sit across from him, but she looked as if she were choosing her words carefully. "You said Ben came to the hotel this morning."

"He did." Alec tried to keep all emotions from his face, though he couldn't quite ignore the surge of anger at the thought of Ben Carnell. It brought back memories of his father's abusive behavior.

"Did you tell him I was here?" There was a note of fear in Sarah's voice, and her gaze drifted downward.

He shook his head. "Dawson and I told him you checked out of the hotel and took a cab. You should be safe for another night or two."

She reached for a pencil-thin breadstick, and he noted the slight tremor in her fingers. "Thank you." Despite the words, her eyes held a fear so deep, it made him uneasy. "Was there anything else you wanted to see me about?"

"There is." He kept his voice neutral, recognizing her fear. "Jasmine told me you didn't have lunch, and I thought we could talk over dinner."

"Do you always invite your housekeepers to dinner?"

"No," he answered honestly. There was no mistaking the wariness in her voice. And normally, he wouldn't place an employee in this position. He didn't want her to feel obligated or threatened in any way. However, in this case, her very presence could threaten the business deal.

"But your circumstances are different than everyone else," he continued. "You are running from abuse, aren't you?"

She took a sip from her water glass and reached for a second breadstick, studying it as she chose her words. "I'm grateful for the job and for a place to stay. But while I appreciate the gesture, I can't let you choose clothes for me."

He reached for his own glass. It wasn't meant to be inappropriate, but he understood why she would think that. He'd asked Cora to pick out some clothes and have them delivered to Sarah's room. At the time, he'd only been thinking of necessities, but his front desk clerk adored shopping and was only too glad to spend his money. "You have nothing else of your own."

"I have my sweatshirt and jeans. Or I can take the money I earned today and buy something from a thrift store. If you don't buy clothes for Jasmine or any of the other housekeepers, you shouldn't do it for me."

He understood her annoyance, but everything about this situation was different. "Jasmine isn't married to Ben Carnell, one of the most powerful businessmen in New York."

Her face remained shielded, and she snapped the breadstick in half. "How well do you know Ben?"

"Our paths have crossed a time or two," he hedged. It wasn't a good idea to reveal too much about his impending business relationship—especially given the circumstances. "But I'll admit, I'm surprised that I never saw you with him." He *had* seen the man out with several other women, however, a fact that he wouldn't disclose. She'd endured enough.

"Ben wanted to protect our privacy." She took a sip of water and then met his gaze. "I appreciate your help, Mr. Harrow. But I can take care of myself and buy my own clothes."

"If that were true, you wouldn't be here now." The words weren't kind, but they were true. He wanted to help her, but he couldn't do it unless she set aside her pride.

She took a sip of water, but her face was as pale as the cloth napkin. "I don't understand why you're helping me. This isn't your fight."

Alec debated what to tell her. He couldn't reveal that he was involved in business dealings with her husband or she would only think he was using her. In her eyes, he saw the broken fear that mirrored his own past. He knew what she was feeling. The helplessness. The sense that every decision was the wrong one. And the inherent doubts that overshadowed everything else.

Instead, he gave her abbreviated version of the truth. "I knew someone who suffered, just as you have. And I couldn't save her."

At that, she raised her eyes to his. He didn't bother hiding any of the pain he'd felt, and for a moment, there was a connection between them. Her eyes were shining with unshed tears, but she gathered her strength, and murmured, "So you're trying to save me, instead."

"I'm only doing what I wish someone had done for her. If you don't want the clothes, don't take them." He finished by saying, "If you don't want the job, you can leave at any time. It's your choice."

One of the waiters saved Sarah from answering by telling them about the evening's specials. Alec ordered a bottle of Prosecco and an appetizer of assorted cheeses and olives. Sarah ordered iced tea and a Caesar salad. When the drinks arrived, she studied him again and said, "I apologize if I misinterpreted your generosity. But you must understand how it seemed."

"It wasn't my intention to make you uncomfortable. I only thought you might need more clothes to wear, since you arrived with nothing. If you want to send them back and exchange them for something else, go ahead."

She eyed him with open suspicion but said nothing. "I'm thankful for the gesture. But… I don't want you to get the wrong impression about me." She took a sip of the iced tea, as if steeling herself. "I'm a married woman."

Did she really think he was expecting her to offer herself in exchange for the charity he'd given? The idea was appalling. "I would never ask that of you or any other employee. Besides that, I'm leaving for France in a few days. We won't see each other again."

She visibly relaxed at his admission. For a long moment, she seemed to be thinking about what to do. "I am grateful for your help in avoiding Ben."

He gave a nod, uncertain of what to say. An awkward silence stretched between them before she finally said,

"Would you excuse me for a moment? When the waiter returns, you can tell him that I'll have the filet mignon in Béarnaise sauce, cooked medium." Without waiting for him to answer, she stood and pushed her chair in, departing the restaurant. He wasn't certain why she'd left, but when the waiter returned with the appetizer, he gave her order, as well as his own.

Sarah returned in fifteen minutes, this time wearing the black trousers and the blue silk blouse. She'd pulled her hair out of the ponytail and the blond strands had a natural wave as they tumbled across her shoulders. Despite the bruise on her cheek, she had her own inner strength that he admired. Sarah Walsh was a survivor.

Her salad was waiting for her, and she smiled as she sat down. "The clothes fit. I'll pay you back for them, once I get my finances sorted."

He had no intention of taking her money, but a nod was the easiest response. He raised his glass of Prosecco in a toast. "To freedom."

Sarah echoed the toast and clinked his glass. After she took a small sip, she began eating the salad, savoring each bite. With a rueful smile, she added, "It's better than the potato chips and candy bar I was planning to eat."

Her ability to maintain a sense of humor amid this crisis was admirable. If she weren't already uncomfortable with his earlier gesture, not to mention married, he might have told her that she looked beautiful. But he wouldn't cross that line. Instead, he wanted her to have a decent meal, clothes to wear, and a chance to feel safe.

"The clothes suit you." He saw the moment her expression faltered, as if she believed he was hitting on her. To counteract it, he said, "I hope today wasn't too difficult for you."

She shook her head. "Jasmine was very helpful. And it was good to be busy…to keep my mind off the situation."

"Do you want me to call a women's shelter for you?" he offered. "Or you may also consult with my attorney, if you like."

She toyed with her salad a moment and then set the fork down. "I appreciate all that you've done for me, Mr. Harrow. But I know I'll have to face Ben sooner or later. I'd rather wait until later."

Their entrees arrived, and for a time, they spoke of mindless topics. He learned that she had a degree in interior design, but she'd never had the chance to use it. "Ben cancelled my interviews," she admitted. "He didn't want me to work."

"And you've lived here ever since your marriage?" he asked. When she nodded, he asked, "Did he ever take you out to L.A.?" Most of Ben's business dealings were based out of California.

"No, he never did. He flies out there often." Her expression softened. "It was always more peaceful when he was gone. I felt like I could breathe again." She sliced a piece off her meat and added, "I never thought when I married him that it would be like this."

"Do you have any family nearby?"

She shook her head. "My brother lives in Florida, but we haven't spoken in years. My mother died of cancer, and my father died in a car accident when I was ten." With a shrug, she said, "So it's just me, myself, and I."

"Don't you have friends in the city?"

"I had friends back home, but I didn't know anyone here. I went to a small college in the Midwest, and I met Ben there a few months before I graduated. He had some business in Columbus, and we dated while he was in town." She finished her glass of Prosecco. "He claimed he wanted to spend all his time with me, since he was only there for a month. We had a whirlwind romance, I guess you could say. I could tell he didn't like it when I went out with friends. After a while, I stopped going. And they stopped asking when I kept saying no."

She spoke in a matter-of-fact tone, as if she were used to the isolation. "It's all right, Mr. Harrow. I'll save the money I earn in these few days, and I'll go to a homeless shelter if I have to."

A part of him knew that if he let her walk out and Ben found out about it, his business deal would burn into ashes. But if he picked up the phone and told Ben Carnell where she was, Harrow Suites would have millions of dollars in profits for the next three years.

All he had to do was throw an innocent woman back into the arms of an abuser. And God help him, he knew he could never do it.

CHAPTER THREE

The second day of work passed swiftly, and Sarah inhaled a bag of chips and a candy bar from the vending machine for dinner. Alec had left another envelope for her at the front desk with cash inside, and she was being careful to save as much as possible. Even after a hot shower and television, she felt restless. She tried to fall asleep on the bed, but no matter how she twisted and turned, she couldn't get comfortable. Despite having more money, she knew better than to imagine that she could stay here indefinitely.

Soon, she might have enough to buy a train ticket to Florida to see her brother. But Christopher might turn her away. Last year, he'd asked to borrow money after he'd been laid off, but Ben had refused to let her help him. She'd sent Christopher a check anyway…yet he'd never cashed it. When her husband had found out, Sarah had paid the price for her defiance.

She rubbed at her bruised cheek, wishing her inner fears could heal as easily. *You have to find a better job.*

And it was time to start looking for a room to rent.

The phone rang, and she jolted from the bed, her heart racing. *Don't answer it,* her brain warned. *It could be Ben.* Though she tried to take deep breaths, the panic swelled inside her with the force of a tidal wave.

He can't hurt you now. Alec sent him away. But despite the logical reasons, she couldn't bring herself to take the risk.

It rang six times before it went to voicemail. Even then, she gripped her fingers in tight fists, feeling sick to her stomach. The flashing light on the phone revealed that the person had left a message, but she could barely bring herself to check it.

Just do it. You have to know if it's him.

After she dialed the number and waited for the recording, she heard the familiar sound of Alec's voice. Her panic calmed, and she sank back into the pillow, so glad it wasn't Ben calling.

"Hi Sarah, this is Alec Harrow. I've arranged for you to gain access to your bank account and personal belongings in the morning," he said. "I made some calls on your behalf."

There was a click, and the message ended. She hung up the phone, wondering why Alec was still helping her. She was a stranger to him, and there was no reason for him to give her so much. She couldn't help but wonder if there was something more going on.

She knew so little about him. Her mind turned over the mystery, even as she donned her maid's uniform and grabbed the room key card. The business center was open twenty-four hours, and she wanted to find out more about Alec Harrow.

Sarah closed the door behind her and went down to the elevators. Once she had access to a computer, she might be able to find out the answers. Some of his questions had brought a sense of uneasiness.

When she reached the ground floor, she walked toward the business center and used her key card to enter the room. The computer was already on, and she accessed the Internet, searching his name.

Most of the information was what she already knew—that Alec was the owner of Harrow Suites, a self-made billionaire. He managed properties across the world, and she ran across a few photographs of him with supermodels at various galas.

He had never married, it seemed. But she stopped scrolling through the photos when she saw a picture of her husband, who had apparently attended one of the same events.

Her jaw tightened as she clicked the photo and brought it to a larger size. Though her husband was standing in the background, there was a beautiful woman on his arm, a brunette wearing a royal blue strapless gown. Ben was leaning in, laughing and kissing her cheek. The woman wore a diamond bracelet on her left arm, and a large wedding ring adorned her finger. The date of the photo was two months ago.

It was his ex-wife, Miranda.

She recognized the woman from a few older pictures Ben had kept around the apartment. Hot anger rose within her, followed by a sickening feeling in her stomach. Her husband had been cheating. There was no doubt of it from the way Ben was smiling at her. The caption mentioned a Los Angeles art gallery opening.

He had taken Miranda to a public gathering with media present, while he'd insisted that Sarah wasn't ready to face the media. But why would he flaunt her in front of everyone?

She was torn between wishing she'd never searched the Internet and wishing she'd searched it sooner. She'd been unprepared for the cold rush of anger that blasted through her. Not only had Ben abused her, but he'd also been stringing her along.

Her face burned with humiliation. He'd never taken her to any public events, claiming that she wasn't ready for the paparazzi, and if she said the wrong thing, she might embarrass him. That had stung, but still, she was his wife. It wasn't so hard to wear an evening gown and sip champagne, behaving like a quiet listener.

Now, she realized that he didn't want anyone to know who she was. Ben had taken her to dinner parties with a few clients, but usually the dinners were hosted by one of his friends or at their own house. There was never any media presence anywhere they'd gone. He'd done everything in his power to keep her hidden.

Her gut tightened, and she was starting to wonder if there was more that he hadn't told her. The uneasiness encircled her, making her wonder if there were other women besides his ex-wife. For all she knew, Ben could have had a different woman in every city. And he traveled often.

She did another Internet search on Ben Carnell. The initial search only brought up his company's webpage, Venture Enterprises. She scrolled through a few pages, but there was nothing beyond the company profile and a few articles interviewing him.

The second time, she did an image search. The first dozen photographs were of Ben meeting with high-profile clients. But as she scrolled through more pages of pictures, she saw his ex-wife standing in the background. Some of the dates were from years ago, while others were more recent.

She could already imagine the confrontation if she dared to say anything to Ben.

Of course, she was there. We were married years ago, and we're invited to the same events. I can't exactly ignore her, can I?

He would find dozens of reasons why she was wrong. *I would never cheat on you,* he'd say. *You're being stupid. How could you think I'm that kind of man? I have to be polite.*

The air in the business center felt stifling. She'd never thought to dig up information on Ben. Two years ago, she'd fallen for his flattery, dazzled by his wealth and power. It had never occurred to her to investigate the man she'd loved.

Sarah shut down the computer, telling herself it didn't matter. Even if he'd been cheating, she wanted out of this marriage. He could have a hundred mistresses if he wanted. As long as she became his ex-wife, it wasn't important.

But the hurt balled up inside her, making her wonder what was wrong with her. She'd tried so hard to change herself, to somehow be the perfect wife for him. But no matter what she did or said, it was never enough.

She stood and pushed the chair in, leaving the business center. It was nearly midnight, and she ought to get some sleep before work tomorrow. But she was still restless, unsettled by what she'd found. She wandered into the lobby and smiled at Cora. The front desk clerk returned the smile and said, "Did you need anything?"

"I'm fine, thanks."

But Cora interrupted, adding, "I hope you liked the clothes. Mr. Harrow let me pick them out, and I thought that color would look great on you."

She stopped a moment and turned back. Before she could ask anything else, Cora said, "He told me to buy you something nice. I hope it was all right?" She offered a friendly smile, and Sarah tried to return it. It did make her feel better to know that Alec had been telling the truth.

"The blouse was gorgeous. Thank you."

"I do love shopping," Cora sighed. With a wink, she added, "But it's more fun when your boss is paying for it."

"I agree." She nodded her thanks and went over to the beverage station to make herself a cup of tea. She didn't want the extra caffeine, so she chose an herbal tea and filled the paper cup with hot water. After stirring it, she glanced up to see Alec returning. "Don't you ever sleep?"

"I can sleep when I'm dead." He chose a paper cup and filled it with coffee for himself. "Do you want some food? We might have cookies left over from the complimentary reception."

"No, that's okay. I should probably go back to my room." She didn't want to linger because he was entirely too easy to talk to.

"Did you get my message about tomorrow morning? I'm sure you need access to your accounts." He stirred creamer into his coffee, and she wasn't certain how to respond. Though she was grateful for his help, it also felt somewhat intrusive. This was her mistake, and she needed to fix it on her own. If she could just get her driver's license from home, the bank would have to give her access to her account.

"I got your voice mail." She sat down in the wingback chair and faced him. Though she ought to tell him to stay out of her business, she couldn't bring herself to say it. He was trying to help, and she didn't want to seem ungrateful. Instead, she deflected the subject and said lightly, "I'm working tomorrow, and I can't afford any time off. I have a tough boss."

Alec caught her irony and shrugged. "You can work extra hours to make up for the time off." She raised an eyebrow and he corrected, "Cleaning, I mean. There are always rooms to clean."

He sat down across from her and took a sip of his coffee. Sarah knew she ought to go, but there were too many questions burning inside her. "May I ask you a question?"

"Go ahead."

A part of her didn't want to know the answer, but she felt the need to ask. "I saw a photo of you online at an art gala in Los Angeles a few months ago. My husband was there."

His face was completely impassive, revealing nothing at all. "There were hundreds of people there."

"There was a woman with him." Her voice had a hard edge to it. "Miranda was her name. What was he…doing with her?"

His face remained neutral, like granite. "There are

some questions you don't want to know the answers to, Sarah."

He was wrong. A wrenching pain twisted her gut with humiliation. She had done everything possible to please Ben, and it was never enough. Now, she knew why—it was because he had gone back to Miranda.

"I do want to know," she said quietly. "Were they romantically involved?"

Alec shrugged, but he met her gaze with a steady look. She set down her tea, feeling both nauseous and furious. How could he do that to her? After all she'd done to try to give Ben a wonderful home, a quiet life away from the media, he'd gone to someone else. And worst of all, he'd punished her when she'd dared to stand up to him only a few days ago. She'd been terrified of his rage, never expecting such a reaction, but now her fear had transformed into something else—a slow burn of anger.

Her emotions gathered into a tight ball, and she leaned back in the chair, not really knowing what to say now. Her gut burned with humiliation, and she had the reckless desire to break into the minibar in her room and drown her sorrows with alcohol. Or chocolate. Or maybe both after she screamed at the top of her lungs.

But maybe the best vengeance was to regain some of what she'd lost. Even if that meant getting help from another powerful man.

She knew better than to trust Alec Harrow, and she didn't fully believe him when he had offered to help. There was another reason, something that ran deeper. He wanted something from her, but she couldn't say what it was.

Possibly it was redemption for the other woman he'd neglected to save.

The thought was sobering. She sensed, without asking, that the woman had died from the abuse.

She did need help right now. There was no one in the city to help her, and she saw no choice but to accept what he was offering. She just had to be careful to maintain the boundaries between them.

"You said you could help me get my personal belongings," she said slowly. "How would I do that? Ben could come home while I'm packing." She didn't like to imagine the confrontation if that happened.

"When he was here yesterday, he mentioned that he had an important meeting this afternoon at his office. I could have someone ensure that he hasn't left yet."

She pondered that for a moment, knowing it was a risk. But if there was a way to move her belongings and get the money and identification she needed, this was her best option.

Alec added, "You should have plenty of time. My driver will take you there so it's safe. I can even send a private security guard with you as an escort."

It was too much. Hiring a guard went above and beyond her fragile boundaries. She was torn by wanting to push him away and refusing...and recognizing her vulnerability. The thought of seeing Ben again terrified her. He had a gun at home, and her heart pounded at the thought of him using it.

You have to put aside your pride and accept the help. There was no other choice.

"Thank you," she managed to say. She held back the

urge to ask him why he was doing this, when the truth was, it didn't matter.

Sarah stood from the chair, and he caught her hand. Her first reaction was to pull away, to flinch at the touch. But she forced herself not to move.

Alec didn't do anything else except hold her hand in his. She felt like a wild animal caught in a trap, but he didn't press for more. After a moment, she grew aware of the heat of his palm and the strength of his fingers. She glanced back into his ice blue eyes and found herself transfixed by the reassurance of his gaze. "It will be all right, Sarah. I promise you that."

She wanted to believe him. But he exuded a confidence she simply couldn't feel right now.

The car pulled in front of her building, and Sarah felt the icy fear freezing through her veins. The doorman, Ellis, stood outside with a scarf covering half his face. He wore the familiar gray coat and a hat, but there was no mistaking his authority. He wouldn't allow anyone inside who wasn't a resident or an approved guest on the list.

"Ms. Walsh, I'll let you off here and circle the block," the driver said.

Sarah thanked him, wishing she had another coat other than the light windbreaker she'd brought that night. She wore the silk blouse and black trousers, hoping Ellis would allow her inside with no questions asked.

True to his word, Alec had sent along a bodyguard to watch over her. Jordan Wilson was built like a linebacker. He opened the car door for her and when she stepped outside, she prayed that Ellis wouldn't stop her.

"Good morning, Ellis," she greeted him. "How is your grandmother doing?" She had baked banana bread for his family last week after his grandmother had broken her hip.

"Much better, Ms. Walsh." His face cracked in a broad smile before it faltered at the sight of the bodyguard. "She got out of the hospital three days ago." He opened the door for her, but hesitated before allowing the bodyguard in. "Do you want to step inside out of the cold?"

"I'm just here to get a few things," she admitted. "I won't be long."

Ellis sighed and folded his arms. "I'm supposed to call Mr. Carnell, you know. He told me you would return."

She nodded but turned her cheek so Ellis would get a good look at it. The bruise had darkened into a sickly purple hue. "I just need my purse and some clothes, that's all." Sarah raised pleading eyes to him. "You didn't see me."

Ellis was already reaching for the spare key. "You can go up but not him." He eyed the bodyguard as if he were a threat.

"My job is to protect Ms. Walsh," Jordan countered. "I go where she goes."

But she already knew she was pushing her luck by being here. "It's fine, Jordan. No one is in the apartment now." At least, she hoped not.

The two men were at a standoff, but she took the key from Ellis and walked over to the elevator. Though she tried to pretend as if everything was normal, she felt herself slipping back into the shadow of the woman she'd been.

Even when she unlocked the front door, the scent of Ben's cologne struck her hard. His presence was everywhere, from the shoes left by the couch, to the dirty mug in the sink.

Her purse was on the coffee table, and he'd taken everything out as if to inventory the contents. Her gut twisted, for he would know she'd been here if she took the purse. Instead, she picked up her driver's license, staring at the picture of her younger self.

Part of her was grateful that he hadn't wanted her to change her last name. After a divorce, it would make it easier to return to the life she'd had. The thought was reassuring, and she picked up her ATM card next. She rearranged the contents of her purse so it didn't look as if anything was missing. Last, she tore off a check from the back of her checkbook. At least she would have that.

Sarah pocketed the identification and went into their shared bedroom. She opened the dresser drawers and then it struck her that she was behaving like a coward again. So what if Ben knew she'd been here? These were *her* things. She had the right to take everything that belonged to her while she could. There was no sense in worrying about it.

Hastily, she grabbed a suitcase and shoved everything inside, stuffing shoes in the outer zipper compartment. She put on her heaviest coat and tucked a hat and gloves into the pockets. Then she opened the safe and pulled out her birth certificate, social security card, and passport.

Last, she returned to the coffee table and put everything back in the purse, including her cell phone which was off. She dragged the heavy suitcase out of the bedroom and took a quick look around to see if she'd missed anything. It was then that she noticed a piece of paper with a printed photograph on it.

The photo was grainy, but there was no doubt it was her. She was wearing the housekeeping uniform, and she'd been emptying the trash can in front of the hotel door. The date on the photograph was yesterday.

Her stomach twisted with nausea. He knew where she was. There was no denying it anymore. She couldn't stay at Harrow Suites any longer because Ben would find her.

Sarah dropped the photograph, telling herself it didn't matter. She would find a way out and soon. She pulled the purse strap over her shoulder and wheeled the suitcase to the door. Then she walked out into the hallway and locked the door behind her.

Downstairs, she returned the key to Ellis. His face was haggard, but he said, "You know I have to call him, or I'll lose my job."

"I know. Just give me an hour—that's all I ask."

He nodded, and on impulse, she gave him a hug. "Give your grandmother my best. And take care of yourself, Ellis."

"You do the same, Ms. Walsh."

Jordan carried the heavy suitcase out to the waiting car. It had begun to snow again, but she was grateful for the warmer coat. As they pulled away from her building, she felt as if she were leaving a part of her former self behind.

And somehow, she would reach for the life she wanted.

"I know you've been helping her," Ben Carnell said, after they wrapped up the meeting. Alec steepled his hands together, wondering how to respond. He didn't bother asking who Carnell was referring to. He also knew that Sarah was safe for the time being, but his choice of words could affect the deal.

If Carnell agreed to the contract, Venture Enterprises would use Harrow Suites exclusively for their travel needs during the next five years. He had negotiated a fair price, and they would meet again after the holidays to finalize the details if all went well. But Ben could end the deal at any time. Alec didn't want this situation to jeopardize everything he'd worked for.

For the time being, he would feign ignorance. "Helping who?" he asked as he reached for a pen.

Carnell sent him a knowing look. "Sarah. I hired a PI to trace her, and she was at your hotel yesterday wearing a housekeeping uniform." Ben sighed and shook his head in disbelief. "Did you think I wouldn't find her?"

"My general manager does the hiring for that property," Alec answered, dismissing the idea. "You can take up that discussion with him. I have thousands of properties to manage, and I don't keep track of employees, any more than you know the names of all your staff at Venture." He closed his briefcase, behaving as if nothing were wrong. "I'll have my assistant arrange our next meeting after the New Year, so you'll have time to look over my offer."

"If she *is* working at your hotel…"

"…then it won't be difficult for you to find her," Alec finished. "It's really none of my concern. My business is with you, not your wife."

A faint smirk caught Carnell's mouth. "I'm glad you see it that way." He stood from the table. "She doesn't belong in a place like that, working as a maid. Though I imagine she'll be ready to come home after a day or two of cleaning."

Alec kept his expression emotionless and escorted Carnell out. Only after the man had gone did he return to his office. He'd learned from his accountant which bank Carnell was using, because part of their contract required that information in order to wire the deposits. Alec took a moment to dial the manager's direct line. Frank Davidson was a friend from college, and he knew his friend could help.

"Alec, it's great to hear from you," Frank said.

After a few moments of conversation with his friend, Alec got to the point. "I have a friend who has a joint account at your bank. I suspect her husband has shut her out of the account." Even if she did get her ATM card or checks from her home, it wouldn't matter. She couldn't access any of her own money.

"I want you to do a favor for me," he continued.

"I can't give you any account information," Frank started to say.

"That's not what I want." He paused a moment and said, "Sarah Walsh is going to try to withdraw money from her bank account today. When she does, I don't want her to know that her husband shut her out."

There was a pause before Frank said, "Go on."

"I'm going to wire ten thousand dollars into an account for her. Let her believe it came from her joint account."

"Her ATM card won't work if he shut down her account," Frank warned.

"I'll have her come in to the branch, and you can give her a new one. Just tell her that there was a malfunction with the card and fix it. Don't tell her where the money came from."

There was silence on the line once again. Finally, Frank said, "What's going on, Alec? What are you involved with?"

"Not what you're thinking," he answered. "But let's just say that I'm not going to turn my back on a woman who's been beaten down."

Frank sighed. "It's your money. But there's something else you should know about Sarah Walsh."

Alec listened for the next few minutes, and a darkening suspicion took root. There was far more to this situation than Sarah knew, and inwardly he cursed Ben Carnell for being a heartless son of a bitch.

"Thank you," he told Frank. "I'll have my accountant wire the money over right now."

And when he hung up the phone, he wondered just how deep the lies went.

After she finished at the bank, Sarah got back into the car, feeling relieved. She had cash now, and enough money to cover her expenses for a few months. The bank manager had met with her personally, and explained that, due to some recent changes, an account number had changed, but she could still access ten thousand dollars from the checking account, though she needed a new ATM card. She suspected that Ben had shut her out of the main account, but somehow there was another account he'd neglected to change. It was enough for now.

The driver continued through the streets, but when they passed Harrow Suites, he kept going. "What's going on?" she asked Jordan.

The bodyguard's expression was grim. "Mr. Harrow called and told us not to take you back to the hotel. He said Ben Carnell was looking for you."

She said nothing, though an icy fear gripped her stomach. Of course. The photograph had proved she was there, and Ben would be sending someone to check the staff members. It wasn't safe anymore.

"Then where are we going?"

"Mr. Harrow has a penthouse near the park," the bodyguard said. "I have instructions to accompany you there. He'll join you as soon as he's finished his business for the day."

Sarah clenched her hands together. A part of her wanted to refuse, for it wasn't Alec's responsibility to become her babysitter. She was a grown woman and could take care of herself. Now that she had access to money, she could go wherever she wanted to. She didn't have to meet with Mr. Harrow or wait around for him.

And yet...she did owe him her thanks. He *had* made it possible for her to retrieve her belongings with a guard to protect her. It wasn't right to disappear now without thanking him. She could wait until he returned home from the meeting and say goodbye. That would be the polite thing to do.

The car pulled in front of a building located in Central Park West, and Jordan opened the door for her. The architecture was beautiful, with an exterior built from beige stone and a classic façade. A large awning stretched over the main doors, and she sensed the tight security of this building from the discreet cameras.

The driver took her suitcase from the trunk, and Jordan spoke with the doorman before they were allowed to enter. She wasn't entirely surprised that the building manager came to greet her, verifying her name and her identification before he accompanied them to the elevator and finally to the penthouse.

When she entered, Jordan brought her luggage inside, and then he started back toward the door.

"Aren't you waiting here with me?" she asked.

He shook his head. "My instructions were to stand outside the door to make sure no one comes inside until Mr. Harrow returns."

With a nod, he departed and closed the door behind him. She had the image of him standing guard, like a medieval sentry. And it *did* make her feel safer.

A ginger cat came trotting down the hallway to greet her, and Sarah smiled, bending down to pet the animal. The cat nudged her ankle before continuing toward the kitchen.

The penthouse was immaculate with windows that offered an amazing view of the cityscape. It was starting to snow again, and she stopped to watch the flakes drifting down upon the balcony.

She explored the downstairs and saw a Christmas tree in one corner with lights but no decorations. A garland was draped across the mantel of the gas fireplace, and a single stocking hung upon a hook. For some reason, the sight of it made her feel bad for Alec. No one should spend the holidays alone.

Sarah turned on the stereo and found a station that played Christmas carols. It might be a few hours before Alec returned, and waiting around doing nothing wasn't the best use of her time. Instead, she made coffee in the small kitchen that looked as if it had never been used. When she opened the cupboards, she found that he had everything he needed for cooking full meals, but one of the pots still had a price tag hanging off the handle.

She had always enjoyed cooking, and she had a few recipes memorized. After a quick inventory of his food, Sarah decided to bake cookies. She pulled her hair back into a ponytail and tucked a dishtowel into her waistband as a makeshift apron. Though she knew it probably wasn't the best idea to bake cookies for a man she barely knew, she did feel grateful to Alec. He'd given her a place to stay, a temporary job, and he'd helped her get her belongings back. The least she could do was make the man some cookies.

But more than that, it made *her* feel better. Ben had never liked it when she baked, claiming that there were too many calories. The last time she'd made fresh cookies, he hadn't eaten any of them. She'd given most of the batch to Ellis.

After an hour, the penthouse smelled delicious. She had several racks of cookies cooling, and she'd been lucky to find confectioner's sugar and had whipped up some buttercream frosting for them.

She finished frosting the last sugar cookie before she cleaned up the kitchen and brought a plate of them to the den. She set the cookies down on the coffee table and curled up on the leather couch with a blanket. Then she turned off the music and flipped on the television, changing channels until she found the movie *It's a Wonderful Life*. The cat joined her on the couch, and she smiled as she watched Donna Reed and Jimmy Stewart enjoying a honeymoon on a rainy night with a leaking roof.

When the movie was nearly over, she heard the front door open, and Alec called out, "Sarah?"

"I'm in here."

He came into the den, his black woolen coat dusted with snowflakes. Once again, she was struck by how attractive he was. His dark hair made those blue eyes stand out, and he reminded her of a younger Pierce Brosnan. Alec unwound his scarf and removed the coat, tossing it on the back of a chair. He wore a black suit perfectly tailored to his form, and she distracted herself by muting the television.

"I made cookies if you're hungry," she offered. "I hope that was all right."

His gaze flickered toward the plate for a moment, and he seemed surprised by them. "That was nice of you." But he made no move to take one. Instead, he drew closer and sat down beside her. His expression was somber, and she didn't know what to make of that. "Sarah, there's something you should know about your husband."

"Why?" Before he could answer, she added, "Don't worry about Ben. I saw a picture his private investigator took of me at the hotel yesterday. I know I can't go back there, but I was able to get money from the bank today. I'll be okay."

She expected him to agree with her, but instead, he said, "There's a problem, Sarah. I found out something today that I wasn't expecting, though I should have guessed it."

"A problem with what?"

"A problem with your marriage."

She couldn't help but smile at that. "Well, that's the understatement of the year, isn't it?" But something about his expression made it clear that there was more he hadn't told her. She waited for him to continue, and he seemed to be choosing his words carefully.

"I made some more calls today. And I asked some questions on your behalf." His icy blue eyes met hers, and she sobered. Whatever he was about to tell her wasn't good news at all.

"Sarah, the woman you saw in the photograph with Ben Carnell wasn't his ex-wife or even his mistress. She's his legal wife."

CHAPTER FOUR

S arah stared at him in disbelief. "What do you mean?" Her voice had gone soft, barely above a whisper. "He and Miranda divorced several years ago."

Alec sat down beside her and shook his head. "No. He might have told you that, but they never divorced." He'd asked his attorney to pull the information this afternoon. He passed her a file folder. Inside was a copy of Ben's marriage license and several photographs of him attending various events in L.A.

Sarah's expression froze, and she flipped through the papers, as if she'd been sucker punched. "I don't understand. How is this possible?" Her coloring had paled, and she set down the file folder unable to look at it. "He married *me*, two years ago."

Alec hated to be the bearer of the news, but she deserved the truth. Ben had played her for a fool, taking advantage of a girl just out of college. He tried to soften the blow. "Your marriage was never legal. There was no license filed, and there's no record of it anywhere. I'm so sorry." And yet, the words wouldn't make her situation any more tolerable.

She closed her eyes as if trying to gather her thoughts. Marigold moved closer, nudging at Sarah's fingers, as if to offer comfort. She stroked the cat's fur, but he saw her hands trembling.

"I know I should deny it," she said quietly, turning to face him. "I should tell you that what you're saying is ridiculous. But right now, all I can think is that it sounds exactly like something Ben would do."

Alec didn't press but reached for one of the frosted sugar cookies. He'd never suspected Ben would play such a sick, twisted joke on a young woman.

She pulled her hair free of the ponytail holder and set it down. "We eloped and had a small wedding on the beach." Her voice was pensive with a hint of sadness. "Ben hired someone to hear our vows, and they were witnessed by the resort owner. I thought it was so romantic at the time."

Alec waited for her to continue, and when she didn't, he prompted, "Did you ever sign a license?"

She shook her head. "He said he'd taken care of that already, and all I had to do was show up."

"And the marriage certificate?"

"I signed a piece of paper, but for all I know, it could have been printed off the Internet." With a weak smile, she added, "I was twenty-two years old and in love with a powerful man. I didn't know any better."

Sarah reached for one of the cookies and snapped it in half. "I suppose Ben fed me lies so I would be his mistress, completely under his command." Her mouth tightened. "I was stupid and believed him."

"Did he ever introduce you as his wife?"

She seemed to think about it for a moment. Then at last, she shook her head. "Sometimes he brought clients over for dinner, but Ben paid more attention to them than to me. He gave them my name, but he never called me his wife."

"And he never took you out in public?"

"No." He said it was because I wasn't ready to face the media." Her face flushed. "I know what he was doing now. He was hiding me. He probably wanted to see how long it would take me to figure it out." Her fingers dug into the cushion. "How could I be so stupid?"

She directed her attention back to the cat, smoothing Marigold's ears. "I guess I really was as dumb as he said I was."

"You weren't dumb," he corrected. "Only too trusting."

"I loved him," she admitted. "Or, at least, I loved the man I thought he was. Until this past year when I could never do anything right." Her fingers moved up to her bruised cheek, and he decided to redirect the conversation away from her pain.

"What do you want to do now?" he asked.

She lifted her shoulders in a shrug. "What can I do? I can't divorce a man I was never married to." There was a slight catch in her voice, as if she blamed herself for what had happened.

"You can leave him," he said. "And you can get a restraining order if you need one."

"I might." Her eyes gleamed with unshed tears, but she gathered her courage and turned off the television. "I do want to thank you for your help, Mr. Harrow. You've been very kind."

"Alec," he corrected. He knew he had trespassed more than he should, but he'd wanted her to have a safe place to go. "And I want you to know that you're free to come and go as you like. I won't bother you in any way—I would only advise you not to return to the hotel for the time being." It wasn't safe for her there.

"Thank you," she said. Marigold nudged at her fingers, seeking attention, and she seemed to be grateful for the distraction of the cat. "I need to find a place to live," she admitted. "Somewhere I don't ever have to see him again."

He understood her desire to escape and asked, "Do you have family anywhere?"

"Florida," she answered. "My brother lives there." With a sigh, she flipped the blanket back and stood from the couch. "But Christopher hasn't spoken to me in the past year. I don't know if he'd let me come and stay with him."

Alec studied her, wondering what would help her the most. She was so vulnerable right now, her eyes holding back tears. Her blond hair was pulled back from her face in a ponytail, and he saw the faint traces of flour on the blue silk shirt. Flour that she'd spilled because she'd taken the time to bake cookies for him.

He couldn't remember a time anyone had done something like that. Eva had died when he was eleven, and his father had gone to jail. The foster families that he'd lived with over the years had been kind, but none were really the cookie-baking kind.

"If you want to stay here, I have three other

bedrooms," he offered. "Or I'll call a cab to take you to a hotel of your choice." He knew he shouldn't get involved with Sarah. And yet, it dug into his conscience that any man could treat her the way Ben had. She was a beautiful, kind woman who didn't deserve any of this.

"Why did you stay in the hotel if you had your own place?" she asked as she sat down on the couch again.

"When one of my hotels isn't turning a profit, sometimes I can find out why if I stay on the property," he answered. He had tried to keep a low profile, and Dawson hadn't spread the news of his presence around.

"The hotel isn't bringing in many guests, except when there are conventions in town," he said, leaning forward. "We're in a good area, but they tend to choose other hotels. Our prices are competitive, but we can do better."

She thought a moment and suggested, "It's the food. The complimentary breakfast is nothing special."

"I don't know if a hot breakfast would help the profit margin. Our restaurant is meant for fine dining, and it's only open in the evening."

She shook her head. "You don't need a hot breakfast, necessarily. You just need something unique. Something different from an ordinary continental breakfast." She leaned back and thought a moment. Then she stared at the cookies and picked one up, studying it carefully. "What about doughnuts?"

"We already offer doughnuts and pastries," he answered, but she shook her head.

"No, you need something more interesting than what you already have." A smile suddenly broke over her face. "I know what you could try. A doughnut bar." She held out the cookie. "Warm up some plain doughnuts and have a station with different flavors of frosting. Chocolate, vanilla, strawberry. And sprinkles for the children. Let people decorate their own doughnuts. Kind of like an ice cream sundae bar, only with doughnut toppings. Or you could do something similar with the waffles. You can build the cost into the room rate. Let people feel like they're getting something extra."

The doughnut bar was an intriguing idea, and he could envision children getting excited about the concept. "We could try it over the weekend to see if it's successful." He would have to make some calls to arrange it.

"You also need better seating in the breakfast area." She outlined suggestions for different table layouts, and he found himself making notes on his phone. Her ideas were strong, and he welcomed the suggestions.

When the cookies were gone, he asked, "Do you want to get some dinner?"

"I should probably go." She stood up from the couch and glanced outside. The snow had returned, and he didn't want her venturing out into the storm. Not to mention, she had nowhere to stay.

"You don't have to leave," he offered. "We could order a pizza and stay in. I wouldn't mind having company while we watch Christmas movies. And there are plenty of spare bedrooms. It's up to you."

Sarah adjusted a flyaway strand back into her ponytail and tucked her feet beneath the blanket. He could tell she was thinking it over, but she seemed wary of the idea. "I don't want to intrude. You probably need to work."

"I've worked enough over the past few days," he

countered. "I'd rather stay in, watch *A Christmas Story*, and eat pizza and cookies with you."

He hadn't meant to add the last two words, and he wished he could take them back. More doubts shadowed her face. He could easily tell what she was thinking, and right now, her heart was hurting from the discovery that she had never been married. He wanted to soothe her broken feelings, though he knew it was all too raw just now. But he didn't want her to feel uncomfortable or threatened in any way. She'd just learned that her so-called husband had betrayed her. The last thing she needed was involvement with someone else—and that wasn't his intent.

"I'd enjoy the company of a friend," he finished. She still seemed uneasy, so he added, "What kind of pizza do you want?"

She hesitated a moment, as if trying to decide what to do. "I don't want you to get the wrong idea, Alec."

"Same," he answered. "But you were nice enough to bake cookies. The least I can do is give you a place to stay. You may have to lock the cat out. She's overly friendly and might try to take over your pillow."

A faint smile seemed to relieve the tension. At last, she sighed. "Okay. But just for one night."

"Fair enough. Now, what kind of pizza?"

"Anything really. Whatever you like."

He realized she was downplaying her own preferences, so he rephrased it. "If it were your last day alive during the zombie apocalypse, what kind of pizza would you want before you die?"

A slight smile tugged at her lips, and she admitted, "Pepperoni with extra cheese."

He placed the order on his phone and said, "Got it. Now we're prepared if the zombies come tonight."

Her expression softened. "Thank you, Alec. And not just for the pizza."

She was grateful to him for his understanding. It felt as if her entire world had split apart, ripped asunder by the lies. Right now, she felt numb, almost in disbelief at what Ben had done. The very foundation of her marriage had crumbled, and she didn't know what to say or do. The shock seemed to encase her in a sheet of invisible ice, until she forced herself not to think of it.

And despite it all, Alec had stood by her, offering her a place to stay.

Was there an underlying reason why he'd helped her? After all this, she was afraid that Alec would want something more—something she wasn't able to give. The last thing she wanted was a romantic involvement with anyone. And though Alec Harrow was a gorgeous guy, she wasn't ready for anything beyond friendship.

"You didn't deserve what Carnell did to you," he said. "Glad I could help."

"I should have known better. Nothing was normal about that marriage." He'd been so controlling, and unless she obeyed him without question, he lashed out. But she wondered *why* he had even bothered to "marry" her. He was a wealthy businessman who could do whatever he wanted. Was it all an elaborate joke? He'd kept her as a mistress, letting her believe she was his wife. Even when she'd mentioned wanting to change her last name to his, Ben had refused.

"You don't need to change your name," he'd said. "We can deal with that later."

"We've been married almost a year," she had argued. "I've waited long enough to be Mrs. Carnell."

"Then you can wait longer," he'd sneered.

After that, she hadn't argued any more. To Ben, any argument was about winning, and it was pointless to voice her own thoughts. Now, she understood the real reason. There *was* no marriage certificate and never had been any true wedding. Part of her wanted to lash out, or even break something. How could she have been so naïve? She'd let herself trust a man who had only used her. The anger rose up so strong, she closed her eyes a moment, trying to tamp it down. Once again, she let the cold denial freeze out the emotions. It was easier to handle the rage when she didn't think of it.

Alec sat down in the chair across from her, and Marigold hopped up on his lap, snuggling beside him. The sight of the cat eased her tension and was a welcome distraction.

"Don't worry, I won't stay too long," she said. "As soon as I can find another hotel or an apartment, I'll be out of here." The words were as much to reassure herself as him. Though she had no idea where she would go, she didn't want him to feel obligated to help.

"I'm leaving for France in the morning," he reminded her. "I intend to inspect the Paris property over the Christmas holiday. If you want to get away for a while where Ben can't find you, you're welcome to stay here if you like. I'll be gone for a week." He paused a moment and then added, "Or if you'd rather go to Florida to see your brother, I can help you get there safely."

She stopped in front of the glass windows, staring out at the night sky. From this vantage point, the skyscrapers were beautiful, silhouetted with golden light. The heavy glass windows of the penthouse muffled the sounds of the city streets, and she could see the trees of Central Park from here.

"Alec, why are you helping me?" she murmured. "And don't say it's about that woman you used to know. I'm a stranger to you. A nobody."

His mouth set in a grim line, making her feel as if she'd been acting whiny. That hadn't been her intention. She just wanted to understand why he'd felt the need to do so much for her.

"The woman was my mother," he admitted. "I was too young to do anything, and she told the rest of her family that everything was fine. There was no one to help her. I'm only doing for you what I wish someone had done for her."

A weight seemed to lift from her shoulders, for it did seem that he wasn't expecting more in return. If that was the case, then she could accept his help and repay him later.

She was almost afraid to ask but couldn't help herself. "What happened to her?"

"My father killed her after he beat her to death. They took him to jail."

An icy chill ran through her skin. She'd never expected his life to be so dark. And yet, it explained so much. He was using her to atone for his own regrets. "I'm so sorry," she said. There were no words that could heal such a painful experience, but it was all she could manage. Without thinking, she started to reach for his hand before she pulled it back.

Alec didn't seem to notice. "All my life, I've felt like it was my fault. If I had told a guidance counselor at school, or if I'd tried to tell Mom's family, maybe it would have been different."

He leaned back against the couch. "The thing is, Dad could be friendly and charming when he wanted to be. He could say all the right things and make her family believe that Mom was just clumsy. He'd joke about it. And then he'd send them something in the mail— something we couldn't afford—as a gift to prove what a great guy he was."

It sounded like an echo of her own experience. "And then you start to think that you were just overreacting," she said softly. "That he didn't really mean to say what he did. He would be charming and good for a while…until it started again."

Alec gave a nod, and he turned to face her. "I always used to think that if my father was truly abusive, it would be that way all the time. But he strung Mom along over the years until she was too afraid to leave him." His gaze turned more intent. "You got out. I know how hard it was for you to leave. But you don't know how lucky you are to find out that Carnell never married you."

She fell silent, knowing that he was right. But at the moment she felt bewildered and tossed about, not knowing which direction to go. She had to find a job and a place to live…and she wasn't so certain she wanted to stay in New York. And every time she tried to envision her future, the feelings of anger and panic threatened to drown her.

"I suppose it's easier that I don't have to divorce him," she agreed. "But it's hard to make so many decisions during the holidays. You're lucky you can escape to France. I imagine it's very beautiful there." The idea of leaving the country filled her with such envy, but she kept those thoughts to herself.

He came to stand beside her. "If you have your passport, you could come with me to Paris. Stay in the hotel and take a vacation while I conduct my business."

The envy tightened into a true wish. She knew she shouldn't even consider the idea. But then he added, "It wouldn't cost you anything, if that's what you're afraid of. I have a private plane, and I'm staying at the Harrow Suites in Paris. You could have your own room and spend your days shopping or sightseeing."

"No, that's too much. I couldn't," she protested. It was far too generous, but even more than that, she still had the fear that he would want more from her. Or worse, that she would want more from him. Even beside her, she could feel his body heat. A part of her wanted to turn and rest her head against his chest. There was no denying that she was attracted to Alec. And somehow, it was worsened by the knowledge that she wasn't married and never had been.

It was strange to suddenly realize that she had choices. She owed Ben no loyalty whatsoever. He had groomed her, chaining her to a life that was only an illusion. If she wanted to cast off those shackles and go somewhere else, she could.

He regarded her with sincerity. "Again, it costs me

nothing. If you change your mind and want to get away, it's no trouble."

"You just want me to ignore my train wreck of a life and come to France with you?" She shook her head. "There's nothing I can give you in return, Alec. I can never repay you."

He shrugged. "I don't expect anything from you. That's not the sort of man I am, Sarah."

She colored, realizing that she'd offended him. "I'm sorry. I shouldn't have said that. It's just that…it's what I'm used to. Ben never gave anything without a price."

He reached out and took her hand. "You can stay in the hotel and give me your opinions." With a wry smile, he added, "Maybe it needs a doughnut breakfast bar."

She wanted to smile but didn't. The heat of his palm burned through her, making her conscious of his nearness. He smelled good, like a hint of cedar and cinnamon. She faltered at his touch, though it was nothing out of the ordinary.

And yet it was. His kindness, his generosity beckoned to her, drawing her nearer. She liked this man, though she knew very little about him. He had given her hope again, a chance to escape the nightmare of her past.

"All right," she said. "I'll come with you to France."

CHAPTER FIVE

Alec stretched out his feet on the ottoman while Sarah was curled up asleep on the opposite side of the leather couch. His cat Marigold was snuggled beside her, and he didn't have the heart to wake either of them. Earlier, they had eaten pizza, and Sarah had boxed up the leftovers, helping him wash the dishes. He'd reminded her that he did own a dishwasher, but she didn't see any reason for it when they'd only used two plates.

After dinner, they had stayed up late watching Christmas movies. *Elf* was her favorite, and she'd laughed unabashedly at Will Farrell. Then they'd watched *The Polar Express* and part of a Hallmark movie before Sarah had fallen asleep on the couch. He'd never spent much time watching movies with a woman. Usually after a night out with one of his previous girlfriends, he'd taken them to bed, and they'd left in the morning. It was uncomplicated and shallow.

It unnerved him to realize how much he was starting to dislike that. It was far more entertaining to eat pizza at home, watch movies, and snuggle with the cat.

Don't get attached, he warned himself. Sarah had been the victim of abuse, and she didn't need another man in her life right now. It was better to let her go while they were only friends.

And yet, when he watched her sleeping, he wished he could lie beside her.

Instead, he took the blanket and covered her. The barest hint of vanilla fragrance caught his attention, like the sugar cookies she'd baked earlier. If she belonged to him, he would lean down and smooth the lock of blond hair from her cheek. He would kiss her deeply, bringing her body atop his. And he would unbutton that blue silk blouse, revealing her creamy flesh.

He gritted his teeth at the arousal that shot through him. God, he was behaving like a bastard. It didn't matter how much he was attracted to Sarah—she wasn't ready for another relationship. He knew that. As for himself, it was simply the loneliness catching up with him. He hadn't dated anyone in over a year, and he'd felt a connection with her. Knowing that she was not—and never had been—married to Carnell made it that much easier to succumb to the attraction.

Instead, he left her alone and returned to his desk. He'd dropped the file folder there earlier, when dinner had arrived, and now he took the time to go over all the details. But even as he reviewed the contract offer, he couldn't stop thinking of Sarah's false marriage. Ben Carnell was one twisted man to concoct such a scheme. Why would he do it? Was there another underlying reason why he would want to control a young woman? Or was he simply that terrible?

It irritated him that he would still have to do business with Venture Enterprises. But he couldn't afford to turn down the opportunity for the contract. He could sign an agreement with the devil if it meant keeping his hotel properties open. Too many jobs and lives were on the line.

A buzzing noise caught his attention, and he traced the sound back to the kitchen. Sarah had plugged her cell phone in, and the call went to voice mail.

But a moment later, he saw a text message flash on the phone.

You stupid slut. I know you're sleeping with him.

Alec picked up the phone, surprised to discover that Sarah didn't have a security password on it. He saw at least five text messages, all from Ben Carnell. Before he could turn off the phone, a sixth message arrived.

I know where you are. And I'll come find you in the morning.

A sudden suspicion caught him, and he went into her phone's settings and turned off all location services. It was likely that Ben had discovered that she'd taken her belongings. And now, he was tracking her through the phone.

They were due to arrive at the airport tomorrow afternoon. But it would be safer to change the time of the flight to earlier. He owned the private jet, so it would be easy enough to make the adjustment, even if it meant a layover in Heathrow.

He held Sarah's phone a moment longer, though his conscience warned him to leave it alone. It infuriated him that Carnell was treating her like a runaway child. Sarah deserved the chance to get away from him.

It wasn't right to interfere when this was her life, her choices. But neither did he want the man to bother her or make her feel threatened. Alec opened up her phone contacts and blocked Carnell. Sarah didn't need a man like that in her life.

She doesn't need you, either, his common sense warned.

But he told himself that this was about giving her the chance to feel safe. He wanted her to enjoy France without receiving intimidating messages from her ex-husband. And if that meant silencing Carnell, so be it.

Sarah woke up early in the morning with a cat nudging her face. She stretched and glanced outside the windows. It was still dark, and when she checked the clock, she saw that it was 5:00 in the morning.

There was a faint light coming from the hall, so she got up and found Alec in the kitchen.

"Morning," she mumbled. "Sorry, I fell asleep on the couch last night."

"I thought about waking you but you looked too comfortable." He held out a mug. "Coffee?"

"Please." She took the cup, and he passed her the cream and sugar. After a few sips, she started to feel human again. The cat wandered into the kitchen and she asked, "What will you do with Marigold while you're gone?"

"My assistant, Lacey, will make sure she's fed and cared for. Marigold despises the kennel."

"She slept beside me all night," Sarah said. "I never

realized how comforting it can be to have an animal snuggle with you." During the last year, she'd always gone to bed alone. Ben was usually traveling, and when he did come home, he had often slept in a different bedroom. Sometimes she'd felt the sense of rejection, though he'd claimed it was because he had to get up early for work.

"Having an animal in your room can be comforting, except when the cat steps on your face and demands food at four in the morning," he countered. "Which has been known to happen." He reached down and picked up the cat. "When I'm traveling, I sometimes take Marigold with me, but it's not possible when I go overseas."

She finished her coffee and asked, "Do I have time to take a shower before we leave?"

"Of course." He led her down the hall toward one of the bedrooms that had its own bathroom. "I put your suitcase in here last night."

Sarah walked inside and saw a queen-sized mahogany sleigh bed with a pale beige duvet and two pillow shams. She couldn't stop herself from touching the furnishings.

"It's a beautiful room," she said. "It's a shame I slept on the couch. But it was comfortable there, too."

He ventured a smile. "If you don't mind eating breakfast on the plane, it will save us a little time."

It was clear that, despite his assurance that she had time to shower, he was in a hurry. She wondered if Ben had caused any trouble but decided not to ask. "That's fine." She thanked him, and he left her alone.

She locked the door and unzipped her suitcase. For a moment, it seemed strange to go through the clothing the stylist had chosen for her. How had she allowed Ben to eliminate her wardrobe and erase that side of herself? She picked out a pair of tailored trousers and an emerald cashmere sweater, hardly looking at them.

After she was dressed, she brushed her hair and put on make-up to hide the bruise. The foundation and powder helped, and she added eyeliner and a rose lipstick to make herself presentable. It wasn't great, but at least she didn't look like a battered woman anymore.

It was a shame she couldn't cover up the invisible bruises under her skin. She'd been just as responsible for the abuse because she'd allowed it to happen. She'd never stood up to him. Marriages were about compromise, she'd always thought. Only, in Ben's case, it had to be his way all the time.

Her emotions knotted in her gut as she packed up the rest of her belongings and rolled the suitcase into the hall. "I'm ready," she told Alec as she put on her coat.

He took her suitcase for her, and they barely spoke on the way downstairs. The car was waiting for them, and he held the door open for her while she climbed inside. He was giving instructions to the driver when her phone buzzed. A text message flashed on the screen from an unfamiliar phone number.

Did you think you could block me? I know where you are.

She closed her eyes and set down the phone. Alec got inside the car, and at his questioning look, she said, "Ben just texted me."

His expression darkened. "You should change phones and get a new number." He thought a moment. "I have an idea. May I?"

She gave him the phone, not knowing what he intended. Alec took her phone and started adjusting her phone settings. He confessed, "I blocked his number when he texted you last night. I also turned off your location services. But it might be better to let him think he knows where you are. I can leave the phone in my driver's car and let him drive around the city today."

An uncertain emotion caught her stomach, and Sarah chose her words carefully. "Though I suppose you were trying to protect me, you shouldn't have touched my phone. Not without asking me."

Alec handed the phone back to her. "You're right. But when he was threatening you last night, I didn't want him to have that power."

She set the phone down on the seat. "Yet, you decided it was okay for *you* to take that power? What makes you any different from Ben?"

His face turned stony. "Because I've given you choices. If you don't want to travel with me, then don't. Stay in the car, and my driver will take you wherever you want."

She knew she'd offended him, but she couldn't simply behave as if he'd done nothing wrong. This was about setting boundaries.

"I'll go with you," she said quietly. "But in the future, please ask me before you make decisions on my behalf."

He gave a nod, but the atmosphere between them grew strained. Within a few minutes, they arrived at the airport. After she'd shown her passport and they were through security, Alec escorted her up the steps and into his private plane. The sleek jet was spacious with leather seats and a couch that could fully recline into a bed. Chilled champagne and orange juice were waiting for them, and Sarah chose a leather chair.

Alec poured a mimosa for her and held it out. "To new beginnings."

She clinked her glass to his and sipped the champagne and orange juice. The flight attendant offered her breakfast choices and took her order. Alec spoke with the pilot quietly, and then he took a seat across from her. For a moment, he busied himself with the seat belt. But then he met her gaze. "I can arrange for another cell phone, once we reach Paris."

"You don't have to," she protested. "I can get one after I return home."

He paused a moment. "I'm not sorry I blocked him from your phone or turned off your location. Any man who tries to intimidate a woman should be blocked."

"What about a man who takes a woman's cell phone without her permission?" she pressed.

"He was stalking you. You don't need that right now. I won't apologize for protecting you."

She leaned back in her seat as the plane prepared for take-off. Alec's expression held concern, but there was something else beneath it—almost a faint note of interest.

Her heartbeat quickened, for she had no desire to be involved with any man at all, much less another man who wanted to control her life. But from the way he was watching her, his stare became an invisible caress. She pushed back the unexpected flare of her own response and steeled herself. "Is there another reason you're interfering, Alec? Something else you want from me?"

Her words sparked an unbidden response, and his body reacted out of instinct. Damn it all, he was trying to do the right thing by giving her an ocean away from Carnell. But Sarah's voice had a softness to it that allured him. He couldn't deny that there was most definitely something he wanted from her.

"No," he answered. "There's nothing I want."

Lies, his mind chided him. If he could have his way, he would lock the door to the cabin, giving them time alone. He would kiss those full lips, pulling her body into his lap. He would slide that emerald sweater from her curves, baring her until he could have her skin against his.

The physical desire became an unbearable ache of wanting. She didn't belong to Carnell anymore. She wasn't married.

But she also didn't want to be involved with anyone.

The flight attendant interrupted their conversation once they reached cruising altitude, bringing them breakfast. Alec unfastened his seat belt and picked at his own food, while Sarah ate. He watched as she bit into a strawberry, her lips closing over the fruit. Living with this woman for the next few days would be pure torture. He'd told her she could enjoy the vacation as just friends, but he couldn't deny that he liked Sarah. The timing was terrible, and he suspected his business deal with Ben had fallen apart because he hadn't been able to set his personal feelings aside. And if he did have to close several hotels, it would mean hundreds of people losing their jobs just after the holidays.

"You're staring at me," she accused.

"Sorry. I was just lost in thought." Which was partially true. He stood from his chair and started to walk to the far end of the cabin.

"Something on your mind?"

"Just…hotel business," he said. "Nothing you could fix, really."

He reached for his laptop and set it upon a table on the opposite side of the cabin. "I'm going to get some work done. There are movies you can watch if you're interested."

She nodded, and he pretended to be occupied with his laptop while she curled up to watch a movie. It occurred to him that today was Christmas Eve. He'd forgotten the date since he rarely had anyone to celebrate with. Sometimes he bought his cat a gift, which was pathetic. Most of the time, he woke up on Christmas morning with a mug of coffee and an empty Christmas tree.

But this year was different. He opened up his browser and started shopping online. He wasn't entirely certain what Sarah might want, but it was interesting to imagine the possibilities.

She was curled up watching a romantic movie on one of the monitors. There was a softness about her, of a woman who longed for romance of her own. And he wondered if it was possible to help her find a different life, one where she could be safe.

She'd made it clear that she wanted nothing but friendship from him, which was for the best, really. Their lives were too different, and she needed time to get over her ex.

Alec checked his email, but he was fully aware of her

presence. The movie ended, but she sat and stared at the screen for a long time, even after it was over.

"Do you suppose Ben is spending Christmas with her?" she asked. "With his wife?"

Alec closed the laptop, and answered, "Possibly." It was a loaded subject he had no desire to touch.

"Did everyone know he was still married? Was I just that stupid?" She stood from her chair and turned to face him.

"I didn't know Ben well, so I can't really say. I don't recall ever meeting his wife, though I might have seen her a time or two." The man had kept his home life hidden.

"I'm still angry about it. Every time I think of it, I want to punch something," she admitted. "It's hard to just let go."

"No one can expect you to get over it that soon. You were a victim."

She stared outside the window, her expression growing distant. "I don't ever want to be that woman again. I can't."

"It may help to get away from New York for a while," he offered. "You can take some time for yourself and decide what you want to do."

Sarah paused at that and turned back to him. "That's a good idea. I just wish it were that easy." Her shoulders slumped forward, and she slipped off her shoes, drawing up one knee. "I keep trying to block him out of my mind. I want to imagine that I can just move on with my life and act as if our relationship never existed. That it doesn't matter what happened before."

"You won't forget what happened," he acknowledged. "But you won't make the same mistake again."

"I know," she agreed. "I tell myself over and over that everything will be different now. And yet, I'm still afraid. Ben doesn't make idle threats."

Alec wasn't about to let anything happen to her. "What do you think he'll try to do?"

"Stalk me," she admitted. "He already traced my phone once. Even though we left it in your car, I think he could find me easily enough."

"You'll be safe," he said quietly. "I won't let anyone get to you. I promise."

She traced her fingers over one of the leather seats. "And yet, here I am, flying to Paris with a man I barely know. I've hardly curbed my impulses."

"Merry Christmas?" he offered.

At that, she sent him a rueful mile. Her eyes warmed with humor, and she added, "I suppose you're right. I have a lot to be thankful for, and I have no reason to feel sorry for myself. I'm away from Ben, and I'm on a plane to Paris. There will be time to think of the past later."

Sarah leaned back in her seat, and her gaze drifted to the window. He didn't press her for more, but he'd meant what he said. Though a part of him knew that he was compensating for what had happened to his mother, he wanted her to feel at ease. And yet, he knew it would take a while for her to feel safe again.

"I'm glad you're here," he admitted. "I haven't spent Christmas with anyone in a long time."

She couldn't quite smile, as if the words had made her nervous. Though he hadn't meant the words to sound stifling, he could understand why it had made her uncomfortable. But once spoken, he couldn't exactly take them back. Better to just leave it alone.

The flight attendant brought lunch to them, and Sarah seemed grateful for the distraction. She thanked her for the roast chicken, mashed potatoes, and steamed vegetables. They ate, and he poured her a glass of white wine.

"I've never been to Paris before," she confessed. "Aside from the Louvre and the Eiffel Tower, I don't know what else there is to see."

"Sacré Coeur and the Arc de Triumph," he suggested. "Or you might enjoy a day trip to Versailles."

"That sounds like fun," she said. "And, in return for this trip, I could give you ideas about what to change in your Paris hotel, just as I did in New York." Her eyes held a spark of interest. "I'm great at choosing furniture or designing the interior of corporate spaces."

"I'll keep that in mind." Alec opened his laptop again and logged in to his hotel account. "Do you want a king bed or two queens for your room tonight?"

"King," she answered.

With a few clicks, he set up a reservation for her. "Done. And I wouldn't mind reports if you find any concerns about the property."

"I'll tell you about every speck of dust," she promised. "Will you need daily debriefings?" There was a note of teasing in her voice.

Yet her words conjured up a sudden rise of interest. "I'll give you a key card of your own," he said. "You can come and talk to me any time you want."

Her smile faded, and he caught the flush on her cheeks. He hadn't really intended the hint of innuendo, but it was too late to pull it back. Instead, Sarah changed the subject. "I'm surprised that you're spending

Christmas working. Don't you have family? A sister or a brother?"

He shook his head. "I was an only child. I spend my holidays alone." He hadn't really stayed in touch with his foster families since he'd only stayed with them a year or two before moving on.

"So, you're trying to escape, too?"

Her prediction was a little too close to the truth, though he'd always intended to spend some time in Europe. He simply hadn't anticipated having a companion. "I have to work."

"Even over Christmas?"

He nodded. "Especially then." It was easier to push back the emptiness of the holidays when he immersed himself in the accounts.

"I suppose it's a difficult holiday if you have no family," she agreed. "But you could do volunteer work. Or take a vacation."

It was easier to simply stay busy with the hotels. He liked traveling, and it was easier to make decisions about the properties by visiting each one.

"What about you?" he asked. "Did you spend Christmas with your brother in the past?"

She shook her head. "No, not since before I was married. Ben wanted me to stay at our home, but he usually wasn't there with me." Her expression faltered. "I suppose he might have been with his real wife."

"Possibly." He pushed his laptop aside. "But your Christmas might have been worse if he was home." He very much doubted that a man like Carnell would spend time watching old movies and eating frosted Christmas cookies.

Sarah seemed to consider that and nodded. "True. I don't suppose he would have paid much attention to the holidays with me." She eyed him and asked, "What about you? Were you ever married before?"

"No." He had never wanted a wife or a family of his own. It was easier to forget the past, always moving from place to place. His father was in jail after killing Eva, and Alec had no one else. A part of him wondered if he could ever have a normal life. He suddenly realized that he'd enjoyed spending time with Sarah more than any other woman. And her laughter during the movie last night, with the cat stretched out beside them, had filled up the loneliness.

"This Christmas will be different. For both of us," he promised.

She offered a tentative smile. "It will, won't it?"

Sarah checked into the Paris Harrow Suites and observed the staff, just as Alec had requested. Everything went smoothly, though they did ask for a credit card for incidental charges. She gave them her bank debit card, though she questioned whether Ben could trace it. Her insides tightened at the thought.

The bellman promised to deliver her bags to her room, and she tipped him, choosing to remain downstairs a little while longer.

Alec had deliberately remained separate from her, claiming that he needed to meet with the general manager. In the meantime, Sarah intended to get settled in the hotel. It was Christmas Eve, and though it was early evening, it was already dark outside. There were soft flakes of snow falling outside, and she took a moment to sit in the lobby and gaze at her surroundings.

The gilt chairs had a fairytale-like quality and were surprisingly comfortable. She watched over the people as they entered the hotel, noticing the brightly wrapped presents that several guests carried. It felt strange to know that she hadn't bought any Christmas presents this year. Ben was always impossible to shop for, and she tended to wait until the last minute to find something. Even then, he'd never seemed to care much about what she'd bought. She used to send gifts to Christopher, but he never responded. Last year, she'd sent a card, but again, there had been no reply. He was the only family she had left, and it hurt to think that they had become so estranged. She didn't know if there was any way to fix it.

You could buy something for Alec, her heart suggested. After everything he had done for her, she wanted to repay him in some small way. Especially since he'd said that he'd celebrated Christmas by burying himself in work.

Sarah went to the ATM machine and withdrew money before walking into the hotel gift shop. There were touristy gifts of Eiffel Tower statues, t-shirts, and postcards. She thought about what Alec might enjoy and chose a selection of chocolates and a bottle of champagne. Then she added a deck of cards with kittens on the front. It was silly, but she knew he liked cats.

It cost more than she'd expected, but she tried not to think about the money. Heaven knew, Alec had spent plenty on her, and he deserved to receive presents on Christmas morning.

There was no gift wrap, but Sarah decided she could improvise. She went upstairs to her room and set the packages inside. She was delighted with the large mahogany king-sized bed and the elegant furnishings. It was a small room but quite cozy. The bathroom had marble tile, and she chose towels and a hand towel to wrap up her Christmas gifts for Alec. It wasn't perfect, but she didn't think he would mind.

A knock sounded at the door, and she peered through the peep hole to see who it was. Alec stood on the other side, and she opened the door.

He handed her a small box. "As promised, here's a phone you can use while you're here." Next, he handed her a key card. "1252," he said. "I'm just down the hall. You can go inside whenever you want."

"I'll knock first," she promised. "And thank you for the phone. Do you want to come in?"

"Not just now. I actually stopped by to invite you to join me for a late dinner," he suggested. "It is your first night in Paris, after all. Do you want to go?"

She hesitated, for it was beginning to sound like a date. And yet, it *was* Christmas Eve. They ought to do something special, just to celebrate the holiday. If she said no, Alec would likely spend time with his laptop, going over numbers. He had spent a good hour of their flight doing just that. And the truth was, she did want to see Paris, even if only for a little while.

"All right," she agreed. "But I should change first."

"Is half an hour enough time?"

"More than enough." She couldn't wait to see the city and intended to get dressed quickly.

"I'll meet you downstairs when you're ready."

She smiled. "I'm looking forward to it." And she realized it was the truth. The idea of spending an evening with Alec sounded like fun.

"Me, too." He reached for her hand and held it a moment. The sudden warmth of his hand was electric, as if it were sliding deeper beneath her skin. It wasn't hard to imagine his hands moving lower down her body.

Her instinct was to pull away. Not because she was afraid of him…but because she was afraid of her own reaction. He had been so kind, and there was an intensity that drew her nearer. It made her want to push past his lonely exterior to find the man beneath.

She couldn't deny the thrill of attraction that struck her senses. Alec Harrow had the look of a man who had walked on the darker side of life. He understood what she had endured, better than anyone else ever could. And something about him drew her closer.

Sarah was starting to question whether this dinner was a good idea. *It means nothing. You're just friends.*

After he left, she leaned back against the door, muttering to herself. "What are you doing, Sarah? This is such a bad idea. A rebound guy is the last thing you need."

I am an idiot, she thought, as she dug through her suitcase to find a dress. Though she didn't know if they would be eating in an upscale restaurant or a street café, it was better to be prepared for anything.

She chose a long-sleeved teal knit dress that clung to her hips and a pair of flats. Heels might be too risky with icy sidewalks.

Sarah glanced in the mirror and decided to leave her hair down. She smoothed the ends, staring at the bruise on her cheek. It was fading, but it was still a reminder of Ben. She used foundation to cover up the bruise and set the make-up with powder. She added a touch of lipstick that was a slightly darker color than her mouth. For now, it was the best she could do.

She pulled on a coat and went into the hallway, tucking the key card into her purse. A few minutes later, she arrived downstairs. Alec was waiting in the lobby, and his expression held interest when he saw her. "You look beautiful, Sarah."

"Thank you. I don't know if this is fancy enough, but it was all I had." She followed him outside, feeling suddenly self-conscious about his presence. Though she knew this was only dinner and perhaps some sightseeing, she could feel an unspoken energy rising between them.

Alec spoke in French to the driver, and when they pulled out of the hotel, she was mesmerized by the lights and the reflection along the River Seine. She smiled when they drew closer to the Eiffel Tower, which was covered in lights.

"I thought we could be tourists tonight," Alec said, as the driver slowed down. "I made dinner reservations here."

"Inside the Eiffel Tower?" She was delighted by the idea. But there were hundreds of people standing in line. The car pulled to a stop, and Alec tipped the driver before guiding her toward one of the security guards. He gave his reservation number, and within moments, they were inside an elevator, riding up to the restaurant. She couldn't stop herself from stealing glimpses of the view as the waiter guided them to their table. Alec gave another order in French, and she caught the word champagne. Within moments, the waiter returned with a bottle and he poured glasses for them.

"To Paris," Alec said, raising his glass.

She clinked it and answered, "Merry Christmas Eve." When she sipped at the champagne, the light fizz was delicious. But it was the gleaming lights of Paris that caught her breath. She had always longed to travel, and the city was beautiful. From their seats, she could see a view of the Trocadéro and the Palais de Chaillot. The blaze of lights was enchanting.

This was the life she had anticipated with Ben, one where they might travel together and enjoy a vacation. But he had never wanted to go with her, always claiming that he was busy with work. And now, she sat across from an attractive man who had helped her escape the Marriage that Wasn't.

Her brain warned her against forming any sort of attachments. She knew Alec was only being a friend and he didn't expect anything in return. But it worried her that she might be letting down her defenses too easily. This Christmas holiday was starting to make her yearn for a real relationship, though it was far too soon.

"This is such an amazing restaurant," she remarked, caught up in the dazzling lights of the city. The restaurant was located on the second floor of the Eiffel Tower, and it featured a six-course meal, paired with wines. She could hardly wait to taste the cuisine.

"What did you think of the Paris hotel?" Alec asked after the waiter brought the wine along with a first course of pan-seared foie gras with a parsnip puree.

"I like it," she said, savoring the first bite. "It's as if you took pieces of Versailles and placed the furnishings around the lobby. I wanted to explore, to find the hidden treasures." The chairs, in particular, had been among her favorites. The waiter came and brought the second wine pairing, and after he left, she asked, "What made you decide to build hotels?"

Alec's gaze shifted toward the tall glass windows, as if he didn't want to reveal everything. Then he admitted, "When I was a boy, we didn't have much money. My mother worked at a daycare center, and my father worked on an assembly line. We stayed in a hotel once when we went to Florida. It wasn't a nice hotel, but I remember feeling that sense of escape. As if, for a few days, my life could be different." An enigmatic smile crossed his face. "My father spent most of the time outside of the hotel. He went to a football game in Miami without us because we only had enough money for his ticket. Those hours alone with my mother were some of the best I ever had. And all we did was go to the hotel's swimming pool."

"I know you loved her," she murmured. She could see it in the way his blue eyes softened.

"My mother was a good person. She did everything for him...washed his clothes, folded them the way he wanted. She made him his meals and always waited to eat with him, even when he came home late from work. But it never seemed to be enough."

There was pain in his eyes, but he refused to say more. All she could offer was, "You must miss her so much."

"She deserved better than the life she had." He reached for the champagne bottle and refilled her glass. "So do you."

Sarah distracted herself with the wine, but inwardly, she was reminding herself that his words meant nothing beyond friendship. He was helping her as a means of atonement, nothing more. It wasn't about any sort of relationship or friendship between them. *Don't lower your guard,* she warned herself. *Don't let yourself believe there could be more.*

And yet, why he would go to such trouble? Why would he bother taking her to Paris or going out to dinner at such an expensive restaurant inside the Eiffel Tower? She pretended to look outside at the view but instead saw the reflection of Alec's face. There was no reason for him to bother with her. But he was studying her with an interest that made her cheeks burn.

The second course arrived, and though the halibut tasted delicious, her attention was caught up in Alec. She turned her gaze downward from his face, only to be caught by his tailored suit and the way it stretched across his broad shoulders. Alec looked like a man who worked out often, and she was mesmerized by the light stubble of beard across his cheeks. She imagined what it would be like to touch his face, but immediately pushed the thought back. *You've had entirely too much wine.* The last thing she needed was to let her heart be drawn down the wrong path.

But as the evening continued, she noticed that Alec had stopped drinking very much. His complexion had gone pale, and tension lined his face. Even during the next few courses, despite her attempts at friendly conversation, she sensed that something was troubling him. "Are you all right?"

"I'm just tired. Don't mind me." He passed her the

plate containing the poached pear in rum sauce and offered her a bite. She did the same, sliding her chocolate almond torte in front of him. Sharing the desserts was intimate, and she savored the sweet pear. But he barely touched the torte.

This was more than jet lag, she was sure. The tightness in his mouth revealed a man trying to hide his discomfort.

"Do you want to see the view?" he asked, after he paid the bill.

"I'd love to." But even as he guided her toward the elevator, she was worried about Alec. Once or twice, she caught him closing his eyes as if to push back pain. The elevator opened at the observation deck, and he allowed her to go first. Her light coat was not enough to deter the wind, and she leaned against him as an icy gust froze her fingertips.

"Sorry. It's much colder than I'd thought it would be."

When he started to remove his own coat, she stopped him. "No. You'll only make me feel guiltier if I take your coat. I'll be fine."

Instead, he put his arm around her, drawing her against his side. She welcomed the touch, putting her arms around his waist. "Don't worry this means nothing," she reassured him. "I'm only stealing your body heat."

"I don't mind," he said. But again, she sensed the unspoken note of pain. She was certain that something was bothering him, though he tried to hide it. For a short while, she admired the view of Paris at night. Alec took a picture of her on his phone with the Paris lights illuminated behind her.

"Would you like me to take a picture of you?" she offered, but he shook his head and declined. Likely because he didn't feel like smiling. She didn't know what was wrong, but whatever the reason, he needed to return to the hotel and rest.

"I think I'm beginning to feel the jet lag," she lied. "Would you mind if we went back to the hotel?"

The look of relief on his face was instantaneous, though he kept his answer neutral. "If you like." He made a call from his phone to order the car around, and they went back inside the elevator.

When they reached the restaurant, she took his hand in hers. "Thank you for dinner," she said. "I loved every moment of it."

"You're welcome."

The car arrived, and he guided her inside. Once they began driving, she tried to watch him out of her peripheral vision. The strain was still there, and she caught him rubbing one of his temples.

"Are you as tired as I am?" she said lightly.

"Very. I'll be glad to crash tonight." He leaned back in the car, and their hands rested side by side. She tried to relax, but she inhaled the masculine scent of his skin. Although she tried not to be obvious about it, she was watching him for signs that he was hurting. Once, he closed his eyes and it appeared as if a flare of pain caught him hard. They rode in silence back to the hotel, and she decided there was time in the morning to walk through Paris if Alec was feeling better.

She sensed that the moment they reached the hotel, everything would change once again, like the breaking of a spell. On impulse, she reached for Alec's hand and squeezed it. "I want you to know how much this evening meant to me. I loved the dinner and…just everything."

He squeezed her palm in answer and didn't let go. The touch of his hand upon hers was magnetic, and she savored the silent caress. She hadn't realized how starved she was for affection, even in the smallest form.

Once they arrived at the hotel, Alec guided her inside. Their rooms were on the same floor, and he walked her to her door. "Good night."

She echoed the words, but he still appeared exhausted. For a moment, she watched him return to his own room through the peep hole. Though Sarah told herself that it was likely nothing, a part of her didn't quite believe it.

She showered and changed into yoga pants and a long T-shirt, pulling her hair up into a bun. But after she brushed her teeth, she stared at herself in the mirror, wondering why it felt so wrong to simply go to sleep.

You're overreacting and being stupid. And yet, her gut instinct warned that she shouldn't leave Alec alone. He looked ill, and the least she could do was bring him some ibuprofen. She put a few bottles of medicine into a clutch purse, tucked her key card inside, and slipped on a pair of flip flops. Then she picked up the key card to Alec's room, staring at it. This was such a risk, barging in on him. He might be angry with her for intruding.

And yet…she couldn't walk away from him. There was no question he wasn't feeling well. He had become her friend, and didn't friends look out for one another?

Her decision made, she closed her room door and walked down the hall. His room was one of the larger suites, and she knocked lightly. She pushed back the rise of nerves, telling herself she could leave if he was fine. When there was no answer, she inserted the key card and opened the door a crack.

"Alec, it's Sarah," she murmured. "Is everything okay?"

The entire room was dark, and she thought she heard the rustle of bedcovers. "You didn't seem well when I left. I thought I would come and check on you."

He mumbled something she couldn't hear, so she flipped on the bathroom light to see. Alec was sprawled across the king-sized bed in his boxer shorts, looking as if he'd been knocked unconscious. He let out a groan when she closed the door.

"Migraine," he muttered. "Sorry."

Sarah hurried to his side. Her brother had suffered from migraines when he was a teenager. "What can I get you? I have ibuprofen, or I could find you something else."

"The medicine is in my luggage. Couldn't find it. Too tired to search." His voice was rough with pain, and she was suddenly glad she had invaded his room. There was a short window of time when prescription migraine medicine could break the headache cycle, and she hoped it wasn't too late. After that, his medicine would do nothing.

"I'll find it," she promised.

Sarah rolled his suitcase into the bathroom, not wanting to switch on any overhead lights. She remembered that light and sound were triggers, and she closed the door behind her while she searched. Eventually, she found a bottle of prescription medicine at the bottom of the suitcase. It must have gotten separated from his toiletries. Sarah recognized the drug as one her brother had taken, and she shook a pill into her hand and filled a glass with water. It would still take an hour to ease the symptoms, and it might already be too late to do any good. Even so, she brought it to him.

"I have your medicine," she told him as she sat on the bed. "Here, take this." She helped him sit up, and he sipped the water and swallowed the pill.

"Sorry to bother you."

"After all you've done for me, I'm glad to help you in return," she whispered. "Lie down, and I'll bring you some ice for your head."

She found the ice bucket and lined it with the plastic bag. Then she took his key card and went back down the hall to fill the bucket halfway with ice. Her brother had often made ice packs for the back of his neck.

Within minutes, she returned to Alec's room with the ice. She made an ice pack with another plastic bag, wrapping it in a hand towel. "Try this," she offered, pressing it to the back of his head.

"Thanks." He barely moved at all, and she sat down on the bed beside him.

"Is there anything else I can get for you? More water?"

"No." His voice was still weighted with exhaustion, and she went to shut off the bathroom light.

Before she left, she reached out to squeeze his hand. "I'll let you sleep now."

His fingers curled around hers. "Would you stay?"

She hesitated while her brain reminded her that this was a very bad idea. And yet, she understood that he was in no condition to call out for help if he needed it. Once his migraine medication began to work, he wouldn't even be aware of her presence. Her brother had always slept as if he were in a coma when he was recovering from a migraine. Alec was no threat at all. After all he'd done for her, it was the least she could do.

"If you like." Sarah started to pull away, but he kept her hand in his. With a sigh, she added, "But if you snore, I'm going to kick you."

"Thank you," he said softly. He rolled to his side, keeping the ice pack pressed to the base of his head. She took the other side of the bed, careful to keep her distance. *You're sleeping in his bed,* her brain warned. *It's not a good idea.*

But she silenced the voice, knowing how much pain he was enduring from the headache. Every sound, every piercing light would bring him more pain. Every sense was heightened.

Just as hers were now.

Sarah was fully aware of his bare skin lying a hand's distance away. And though it was wrong on every level, she wished she could reach out to him. She wanted to soothe him, to lie close and feel the simple comfort of his steady breathing.

She closed her eyes and pulled the coverlet over her. Her heart was beating faster, while she questioned what she was doing. There was no denying that she had come to care about Alec Harrow. Not only had he given her sanctuary, but he had given her a reason to smile again.

It wasn't about the fancy dinners or the trip to Paris—it was about watching movies on the couch with a cat between them while eating pizza and cookies. She could be herself around him, without questioning if she was good enough. They had both come from humble beginnings, and she didn't care about trying to impress him.

The problem was, her defenses were falling fast. And while she didn't want a rebound relationship, she couldn't deny her own attraction. She wouldn't mind cuddling up to Alec, feeling warm arms around her while she fell asleep.

With reluctance, she turned away from him and closed her eyes, wondering how she could guard her wayward heart.

CHAPTER SIX

In the morning, Alec rolled over and a light floral scent caught his attention. Sarah was sprawled asleep on her stomach, and her hair was tucked in a messy bun. She wore yoga pants and a T-shirt, looking as if she'd spent the night watching over him.

His head still ached, but it wasn't nearly as bad as it had been during dinner. The migraine had struck ruthlessly, and he'd been so grateful for her help in finding the medication. For a moment, he watched her sleep, marveling at the softness of her face. Whether Sarah knew it or not, she took his breath away.

For a moment, he imagined what it would be like to have this woman beside him. If she were his, he would draw her into his arms, kissing her. The very sight of her in his bed aroused him, awakening the fierce need to claim that mouth and make her burn the way he did.

Was it so wrong to tempt her? Would she push him away?

He slid a fallen lock of her hair behind one ear, and she opened her eyes, turning to face him. For a moment, she looked surprised at her surroundings, but then she met his gaze. Her green eyes studied him, and he sensed the heat building between them. She reached up and covered his hand with her own, saying nothing at all.

It was the only invitation he needed. Alec leaned in and kissed her gently. Her lips were as soft as he'd imagined, and she didn't push him away. Instead, she yielded, as if she wanted the kiss. And the knowledge only flared his desire hotter.

He pulled back, studying her to see if he'd made a wrong move. Her cheeks reddened, but she didn't tell him to stop. Instead, she held his gaze with hers.

Alec kissed her a second time, in an offering meant to entice. He drew his mouth to her jaw, tracing a path to her throat. Sarah shivered at the sensation and reached out to rest her palm on his bare chest. His heartbeat quickened, and the slight touch told him that she wasn't objecting to his invitation. Instead, she seemed curious, almost intrigued by him. She ran her fingers over his pectoral muscles, and his body responded instantly, as if she had brought her hand lower. He didn't want to frighten her, so he didn't press for more. But he yearned to pull her body against his, running his hands over her curves.

His body was rock hard, and the thought of her softness pressed against him was enough to make him grit his teeth. *Get yourself under control,* he ordered. *You can't frighten her. She's been through enough.*

And though he wanted to strip off the barriers between them, kissing her naked flesh, he captured her in another kiss before pulling back. "Merry Christmas," he murmured against her mouth.

She ventured a smile. "I'd forgotten. It is Christmas morning, isn't it?"

Then he glanced up. "Invisible mistletoe. You can't see it, but it's there. That's why I kissed you."

"Oh, okay." Her smile deepened, and he warmed at the sight of it.

"When a man wakes up and finds a beautiful woman in his bed, it would be a crime not to kiss her." *Or touch her.* Right now, his body was rigid, his mind barely keeping it all under control. It took every effort not to drag her atop him, tearing off her T-shirt and tasting that delicious skin.

"I didn't mind." Her voice was the barest whisper, almost shy. The answer only deepened his discomfort, and he shifted beneath the covers. "How is your migraine?" she asked. "You look like it's still bothering you."

It wasn't the headache at all—only the ache of sexual frustration. But he answered, "It's better than last night." Though the headache wasn't entirely gone, the distraction of her presence was making it easier to endure. "I'm glad you came up to my room. It would have been terrible without your help."

"All I did was give you medicine." She let her hand slide back to the sheet, and he took her palm.

"And ice," he reminded her. The cold ice had soothed the massive headache. "You were here in case I needed anything." He stroked her cheek with his knuckle. "It was kind of you."

"I wasn't about to leave you alone. Not when you needed someone to stay." She leaned on her side and regarded him. "Is there anyone working in the hotel today? It *is* Christmas, after all."

"We have a bare minimum staff. Anyone who chooses to work can work a half day at double the hourly rate," he said. "Some of the younger staff members who don't have children are glad to have the extra money."

"Should we go down and look at the breakfast buffet?" she suggested. "I'm getting hungry."

"Room service," he countered. "My head can't take the noise." The truth was, he wanted more time alone with Sarah. He wasn't certain whether anything had begun between them, or whether she wanted to deny it.

"I'm sorry, I wasn't thinking. Good idea." She rolled out of the bed and handed him the menu. "Will you put in the order? I don't care what it is, as long as there's some fruit and coffee." Then she passed him the cordless phone. "Do you mind if I take a shower?"

"Go ahead." He would just lie back and try not to imagine her naked with water streaming over her bare skin. It seemed that this Christmas involved nothing but physical torment.

"Thanks." Sarah grabbed a bathrobe from the closet. "I have a confession to make. I do have presents for you, but they're in my room right now."

"I bought you some presents, too," he admitted. "We can exchange gifts after breakfast if you want."

"That sounds nice." She disappeared into the bathroom, and he called in the breakfast order. While she showered, he found himself wishing he could open the door and join her. He envisioned sliding soapy hands over her smooth skin, making her feel the same desire rising within him.

This was a torture he had never expected. He knew

Sarah was wary of all men right now, and she had a reason for it. But the past few days he'd spent with her had brought him an unexpected sense of companionship. Despite the migraine, he had enjoyed seeing the wonder on her face at the sight of Paris.

He decided to bring out the presents he'd ordered for her. They had arrived at the hotel late yesterday, already gift-wrapped.

He checked his cell phone and saw that he had a few missed messages from his assistant, Lacey. She had texted that his meeting with Carnell would be next week. It seemed that he hadn't abandoned the business deal after all.

Alec sobered at the reminder that there was more at stake than his own personal desires. He couldn't afford to walk away from this option if they could reach an agreement, but Sarah might get the wrong idea if she found out about it.

She came out of the shower with her hair wet and combed back. She wore a white fluffy bathrobe, and he was drawn to the bare skin beneath her throat. "The bathroom is all yours," she offered. "What did you order for breakfast?"

"I asked for crepes," he said. "Also some cheese, fruit, and croissants."

"It sounds delicious." She went toward the chair on the opposite side of the room, and he stood from the bed.

"I'm going to take a shower now." The sheet slid away, revealing his boxer shorts. Her gaze passed over his body, and he turned to hide the effect she had on him. Even so, his mind returned to the earlier fantasy of her joining him in the shower. As he walked toward the bathroom, he remembered their stolen kiss, and he couldn't deny that he wanted more.

Sarah wasn't married to Ben Carnell and never had been. Ben had abused her, tricking her into a false relationship and never treating her as she deserved. Alec was torn between wanting to avenge her for what she had suffered…and wanting to show her what she'd been missing in a relationship.

He glanced back and saw her face flush as if he'd caught her staring. All he had to do was cross the room and take her face in his hands, kissing her deeply. He could claim that mouth again, pulling her body close until he lost himself in her.

The moment stretched between them, beckoning toward something more. His pulse quickened with the need to go to her.

But he didn't want Sarah to feel as if he were forcing her into something she didn't want. Upon her face, he saw uncertainty, like a woman too nervous to move.

With reluctance, he turned away and closed the bathroom door behind him.

Sarah sat up on the bed, her heart pounding. She pushed back the uncertain feelings, not knowing what had begun between them. In the bathroom, she heard the spray of the shower, and the sound conjured images of his bare skin with water droplets spilling down his chest. She bit her lip, forcing the thoughts away. Beside her, the sheets were still warm from Alec's body heat. Sarah lay there for a moment, questioning what she was doing. In the past few days, she had escaped a controlling husband, only to learn that they had never been married at all.

And now, she had spent the night with a man she barely knew and had kissed him. *Don't do this. You know nothing about this man. Don't get involved.*

But she closed her eyes and inhaled the lingering scent of his skin. When he had kissed her, it felt as if every part of her had come alive. Her skin was incredibly sensitive, and she was shocked by how badly she had wanted him. It was as if she were starving for affection. And if she stayed with him, it would only result in bad decisions.

The shower spray stopped, and she was tempted to return to her own room before she succumbed to temptation. But before she could do anything, there was a knock at the door. She went to open it, and the room service attendant greeted her. "Bon matin." Sarah opened the door wider, and he wheeled in a cart covered with a white tablecloth. He spoke in French, which she didn't understand, but she motioned for him to set up the breakfast on the other side of the room. He uncovered each of the dishes, smiling as he presented them, "Voila." She tipped him, and he thanked her, leaving the room.

A moment later, the bathroom door opened, and Alec walked out, wearing a towel. "I should have brought clothes inside with me," he apologized. "I wasn't thinking."

"It's all right. I can turn around while you get dressed." She took a chair and sat facing the wall, while she chose a plate. "But I may eat all your food if you take too long." Her voice came out sounding too cheerful, almost as if she were in denial about the earlier kiss. It would be best if she forgot about it, pretending it had never happened.

She heard the sound of the towel dropping to the floor and a suitcase unzipping. She poured herself a cup of coffee, and suddenly realized she had a perfect view of Alec's body in the reflection of the silver coffee pot.

Do not *look at him,* her brain warned. And yet, Alec Harrow was a gorgeous man. She couldn't help but sneak a peek at him. It was a shame to put a shirt on that body. She realized that in the midst of her distraction, she hadn't chosen any food. Quickly, she used the tongs to serve one of the crepes. She added fresh raspberries and a warm vanilla sauce, quickly eating a bite to make it seem as if she hadn't been ogling him.

"What do you think?" he asked, coming up from behind her.

"It's delicious," she said, only half-referring to the crepes and mostly referring to him. Her cheeks were burning, and she added cream and sugar to the coffee, feeling as if she really ought to go back to her own room.

His hair was wet from the shower, and she could smell the fresh scent of pine and soap. "Merry Christmas," he said quietly. He was wearing a T-shirt and jeans that encased his thighs in an amazing way.

"Merry Christmas," she answered. "Do you want to exchange gifts now? Should I go get mine?"

"You can finish eating first, if you like." He poured his own cup of coffee and took a crepe, along with a warm croissant. "There's no rush."

She savored the breakfast, realizing that this was the

first Christmas she hadn't spent alone during the past two years. Ben had always called her, but they had not shared a single holiday together. They usually opened presents at New Year's, after he returned to New York.

"Thank you for bringing me to Paris," she said. "And I hope your headache is gone."

"There's still a slight pain, but it's nothing like last night," he admitted, before he drained the coffee. He poured a second cup and added, "The caffeine helps."

"I'm glad you're all right now." She finished her crepe, and then stood up. "If you'll wait a moment, I'll be right back with the gifts."

"You didn't need to buy me anything."

"I wanted to." With that, she turned and left his room, hurrying back to her own. When she opened the door, she paused in front of the mirror. She looked as if she'd just returned from yoga class with her hair in a ponytail. Ugh. Not exactly her best look. But still, she couldn't get her mind off the unexpected kiss. Alec had made her feel beautiful, almost cherished. The very memory of his mouth upon hers made her breathless.

Sarah gathered up the presents wrapped in hand towels and put them inside the hotel's laundry bag. When she slung it over her shoulder, she rather felt like Santa Claus. She walked down the hall to his room and knocked, realizing she'd forgotten the key card he'd given her. When he opened it, she said, "Ho, ho, ho."

His mouth twitched with a smile, and he let her inside. Sarah swung the laundry sack from her shoulder and deposited it on the rumpled bed. "I'll go first."

He sat down, and she handed him the square box of chocolates wrapped in the hand towel. "Enjoy."

He took the terry cloth, and said, "Thank you. I think it's the best Christmas present I've had in a long time."

"But you haven't opened it yet."

His blue eyes held hers transfixed, and he said, "It's been a long time since anyone gave me a Christmas present."

Sarah found that hard to believe, but then again, his mother was gone. His colleagues might not have bought him any gifts because he was so wealthy. The sympathetic ache inside her deepened, but she managed a smile. "I hope you like it."

"It doesn't matter what's inside," he answered. "I already like it because you bought it for me."

His sincerity touched her, and she managed a nod. If she didn't push back against her traitorous heart, she would start to care about this man. And it was entirely too soon to let that happen.

Alec unfolded the hand towel to reveal the chocolate. "These look amazing." Then he offered, "I'll share them with you."

"That might not be a good idea. I have a weakness for chocolate, and I lack self-control."

"I don't mind." But he set aside the chocolate and passed her a large, wrapped box with a plaid bow.

"When did you have time to gift wrap this?" she asked as she tore the box open.

"I selected gift wrap options when I ordered it online during our flight." There was a bemused expression on his face. "I can't take credit."

She opened the lid and found an assortment of seasonal cookie cutters, a rolling pin, and an apron. The thoughtful gift made her throat constrict with emotion.

He'd remembered the cookies she'd baked and had tried to choose something she would love. "This is wonderful." Even Ben had never given her gifts beyond the gold watch or gift cards. It made her own presents seem silly by comparison.

"And there's something else." He passed her a small gift bag. Inside, she found a pair of bright red gloves and a woolen hat. "In case you're ever caught walking in a blizzard again."

Her face softened into a smile. "I hope I won't have to do that again. But thank you."

Despite her inhibitions, she forced herself to give him the other two presents. They were hardly worth anything, but it was all she had to offer.

"They aren't much," she apologized. "Just some things I found in the gift shop."

He unwrapped the champagne bottle and smiled. "Your gifts are meant to be shared. Those are the best kind." When he unfolded the washcloth and revealed the deck of cards with the fluffy kitten, he started to laugh.

"You did seem to like cats," she said. "I know it's stupid, but I thought they might remind you of Marigold."

He set the cards aside, and the expression on his face turned serious. "I like all the gifts, Sarah. It means a lot to me that you chose them."

Her heart warmed at his words, but she warned herself to be careful. But when Alec came to sit beside her on the bed, her thoughts scattered. "I want to kiss you again. To say thank you and to wish you a Merry Christmas." He reached out and tucked a loose strand of her ponytail behind one ear. "But I don't want to push you into something you don't want."

His touch burned into her skin, along with the guilty realization that she *did* want him. She wanted to throw her good sense away and let herself fall beneath his spell. The thought of seizing a reckless moment in the arms of a gorgeous man terrified her, making her wonder what had taken control of her good sense. No. She couldn't take that risk.

Sarah decided to be honest. "I liked kissing you, Alec. But I'm afraid it will lead to something I'm not ready for." Her gut twisted with regret and worry, not wanting to disappoint him.

Instead, he merely let his hand slide across her cheek. "Then we should open the champagne and chocolates. We can see if there are any Christmas movies on television, since everything will be closed today. That is, if you want to stay inside."

Her emotions flooded with such relief, she wanted to cry. It did sound like a great way to spend the day, especially if his headache was still there. "That sounds nice. But I should get dressed first."

"If you like." He propped several pillows against the headboard, making room for her. "I'm not going anywhere."

She took her box of kitchen gifts with her and returned to her room. It gave her a moment to clear her head and think about what she was doing. Alec had respected her wishes and would not push her toward more…but he'd confirmed that he was interested in her.

Sarah closed her eyes and took a breath. She dressed in jeans and a sweater, before brushing her hair and slipping on flats.

The new cell phone Alec had given her buzzed, and

she picked it up, wondering if he needed something. There was a new text message, and she opened it, only to see five words.

I know where you are.

❧

Alec had just flipped the television channel when the door to his room opened, and Sarah entered. Her face was white, and she held out the cell phone he'd given her.

"How did Ben get this number?" Her hand was shaking, and she dropped the phone on the bed as if it were a poisonous snake.

Alec picked up the phone and saw the text message. Inwardly, he cursed, wondering the same thing. It was a brand-new phone, only activated yesterday.

Then he recalled that he'd emailed his assistant, Lacey, to arrange for the phone to be there when they arrived in Paris. She knew the cell number because she had ordered the line to be added to his account. Had she given the number to Ben by mistake? He couldn't imagine why else she would have done such a thing. It wasn't like her at all.

Damn it all.

"My assistant might have accidentally given it to him," he admitted. "I'll call Lacey and explain. She probably thought the phone was mine."

Her mouth tightened, and she rested her wrists on her knees. "Why would Lacey think you had any involvement with Ben? You sent him away from your hotel. You have nothing to do with my ex-husband.

Or…whatever he is." She closed her eyes and sat down limply in a chair.

Careful. Sarah knew nothing of the business deal, and he couldn't let her find out. She wouldn't understand why it was so important to keep this meeting—especially when so many jobs depended on it. She would see it as a betrayal.

He'd already compartmentalized his dealings with Ben. The two men were separate in his brain. There was the businessman who could bring stability to his hotel chain. Then there was the abusive stalker that a primitive part of Alec wanted to pound into oblivion.

"Don't answer the text," he said. "Leave the phone here if you want."

She took a breath and admitted, "I don't want to ever see him again, Alec. I want him out of my life forever."

It was clear that her mood had shifted back into fear. But he didn't want her to dwell on it. "I'm sorry this happened."

"Why would Ben even care where I am?" she blurted out. "He's already married to someone else. Why would it matter if I leave him?"

"It's about power and control. He doesn't want you to take back your own life." Alec stood and reached for the champagne. "But you can do whatever you want."

He uncorked the bottle and found two wine glasses near the ice bucket. He poured a glass for her and one for himself. "Ignore the message. Let it go, and don't let him ruin your Christmas."

Sarah took the glass but didn't drink. It seemed that she was considering it. Alec opened the box of chocolates she'd given him and offered her one. She chose a caramel and met his gaze. "You're right. I won't let Ben ruin my Christmas or anything else. I intend to do whatever I want. He has no say over my life anymore."

He raised his glass to her. "Cheers to that."

She clinked his glass and took a sip before she ate the chocolate. She savored the taste, and from the look of longing on her face, he offered her another one.

"No, these are yours," she insisted. But when he continued to hold out the box, she finally chose a chocolate and lifted it to his mouth instead.

Alec froze instantly. Then he ate the confection, fully aware of his mouth against her fingertips. He imagined taking those fingers in his mouth, sucking gently, before he claimed her lips in a kiss.

Though she was fully dressed in jeans and an ice blue sweater that clung to her curves, his imagination peeled off the layers. Would her bare skin feel like silk? He pictured pressing her back into the soft duvet, her curves yielding as she surrendered. God, he wanted to pleasure this woman. He wanted to push back the darker memories and replace them with something better.

He shut the thought down. Sarah wasn't ready and had told him as much. But she deserved more than the bastard she'd married.

The chocolate truffle melted in his mouth, and he took a sip of his champagne. The fizz blended with the chocolate, and then he chose a raspberry from the room service fruit plate. "Want one?" he asked, trying to break the spell she had set upon him.

"Please." She held out her hand and took a raspberry, sitting back on the bed. "Did you find a movie to watch?"

"I'm torn between *Rudolph* and *Frosty*," he said. "Or *'A Christmas Carol.'"

"Oh, let's watch Ebenezer Scrooge," she said. She chose a spot beside him and propped up a pillow. Alec brought the champagne bucket between them, using it almost as a barrier. It was a physical reminder not to trespass. He filled her glass again and set the chocolates between them.

But he wasn't watching the movie at all. He kept his face toward the screen, but he was taking in the details of Sarah's face. The bruise had nearly healed, but every time he saw it, it brought out the desire to exact the same vengeance upon Carnell.

Her green eyes warmed as the Ghost of Christmas Past took Ebenezer Scrooge back to meet his first love. A softness stole over her face, a wistful expression of a woman who dreamed of romance. He wanted to give that to her.

She caught his gaze and asked, "What is it?"

With a smile, he adjusted his pillow. "Nothing at all." But he nudged the cell phone off the bed and onto the floor so there was no chance of another interruption.

She returned the smile and leaned on one arm as she continued to watch the movie. Her blond hair was tousled around her face, and he decided he liked her better when she'd worn the yoga pants and T-shirt. Her natural beauty outshone all the other women he'd dated, and he liked the fact that Sarah could pull her hair into a bun and not care that she wasn't wearing makeup.

His headache started to return, so he took a few ibuprofen pills to push it back. This time, he wanted to be fully conscious around Sarah. She was enthralled by the movie, and he was enjoying her presence.

When the movie was over, she leaned on her side. "How are you feeling now?"

"A little better. If you want to walk around the city, I could probably manage."

Sarah brightened at the idea. "I would like that, yes." She stood up from the bed and stretched. "Should I roll the room service cart into the hall?"

"I'll do it," he offered. "If you could hold the door open for me."

She crossed the room to help him, when abruptly, his cell phone began ringing. Alec cursed and reached for it.

"Don't answer it," she warned.

He didn't listen. If it was Carnell, he had a few words to say to the man. He touched the screen to answer and said, "This is Harrow."

The woman's voice on the other end of the line was unfamiliar. "Hello, Mr. Harrow. I'm sorry for interrupting you on Christmas Day."

"Who is this?" he demanded, exchanging a look with Sarah. Her demeanor transformed instantly, as if she was thankful it was not Ben.

"This is Miranda Carnell. I think you know my husband."

His mind spun off with a thousand questions, but he forced himself to answer, "Yes."

"Are you able to talk right now?" she asked calmly.

"No." He went to the room service cart and started to wheel it outside the door.

"All right then, I'll call again later. But there are some things we need to discuss." She hung up the phone, and Alec paused a moment.

Right now, he wanted to protect Sarah from the storm brewing. Ben's wife would only want to hurt her because of her husband's infidelity. He didn't know what he could do to shield Sarah from what was to come.

But he intended to try.

CHAPTER SEVEN

Sarah knew Alec was hiding something, but she didn't pry. She didn't believe for one moment that it was a wrong number. And yet, when he'd gone to get his coat, she had checked his recent calls and it wasn't a phone number she recognized.

If Alec's assistant had, in fact, given the new cell phone number to Ben, it was probably for business reasons. She didn't want to believe that Alec was arranging any deals with Ben, but she couldn't rule out the possibility.

He had taken care of her, giving her a place to stay, a job, access to money, and even a trip to Paris. What kind of man did that unless he expected something in return? He'd kissed her this morning, and that had most definitely crossed the line of friendship. But in the back of her mind, the suspicions deepened, making her feel wary.

There weren't many people out walking, and she tried to force her attention back to sightseeing as she and Alec continued down the street. There was chill in the air, and all the shops were closed. There were rows of white tents decorated with holiday lights, but the Christmas market had now ended.

They walked in the direction of Notre Dame Cathedral at the far end of the Seine. In the distance, she could see a Christmas tree outside, lit up for the holidays. Alec led her toward one of the bridges, and she leaned against the stone balustrade. The water below was dark with chunks of ice floating near the shore.

Inwardly, her thoughts were churning. She wanted to confront him, but her instincts warned her not to say anything. *He'll just get angry, and you'll ruin this memory.*

It doesn't matter who called him. It's none of your business. She pushed back the urge to demand answers. Instead, she took deep breaths, calming herself. Silence descended between them, and she forced herself to make conversation.

"Is New York your true home?" she asked. "Or do you travel throughout the year?"

"It's the closest thing I have to a home. But I do travel often." He glanced back at the Eiffel Tower which stretched high above the landscape. "It's not a bad life."

"It's lonely," she countered. "With no family, don't you sometimes feel like you're missing something?"

He was quiet for a time. Then he admitted, "I do still have family. My father's been in jail for years now."

Sarah sobered at the revelation and the bitterness in his voice. She'd made a thoughtless remark and wished she could take it back. "I'm sorry for what happened to your mother."

He gave a nod but said nothing else. Then his hand

bumped against her fingers in a silent invitation. Wordlessly, she took his hand. She wanted him to know that he wasn't alone just now. Although she had no idea what would happen between them, or if he had any connection at all to Ben, she *did* want to remain his friend. She owed him that much.

They walked for a distance along the banks of the Seine. She didn't know what to say, but the weight of her suspicion made it hard to trust him.

"Merry Christmas, Sarah," he said at last, stopping near the edge of a bridge. "I'm glad you're here." He took her other hand in his, and her heart gave a leap.

Stop it, she warned herself. *You don't need a rebound affair. Shut that down right now.*

She felt too vulnerable just now, and an affair wasn't smart—especially with a man whose intentions she was starting to doubt. Maybe the best way to handle this was to deflect him. She ventured an easy smile. "It's good to spend Christmas with a friend. It makes it less lonely."

He kept her palm in his. "It's not friendship I want anymore, Sarah." He squeezed her hands a moment before releasing them. "But we both know you're not ready for more. I won't ask that of you."

Her face colored because he'd seen right through her. In the hazy afternoon light, she was caught up by his handsome face. His deep blue eyes held her mesmerized, drawing her closer. There was a faint stubble of beard on his cheeks, and she found herself wishing she weren't so broken, that she could simply steal a moment for herself.

She took a breath and admitted, "You're right. It's too soon for me. But I do care about you. Perhaps more than I should." A part of her wondered what it would have been like if she had met Alec first.

"There's no rush," Alex said. "We can be friends for as long as you want. Or if that's all you want." He pressed his hand to her spine in silent support. His touch brought her comfort, and she found that her tension had begun to ease. For a while, they walked along the riverbanks in the quiet solitude. She wished she could lay aside all her fears and be open to a new relationship. But Alec needed to understand her past first.

"After I...'married' Ben, he changed." She searched for the right words, hoping he would understand. "It was almost like the hunt was gone, and he got bored." She slowed her pace, watching the river lapping at the edges of the large bridge. "I felt discarded. Like a toy he no longer wanted." With a rueful smile, Sarah admitted, "I kept trying to please him. I wore the clothes the stylist picked out for me, and I tried to be the sort of wife he wanted. But it was never enough."

After that, Ben had begun to criticize her. If she chose her own food off the menu, he would berate her if he thought it was too fattening. She had demurred to his wishes, but his moods shifted so often, it was impossible to keep up.

"He only praised me when I did everything he wanted. After a while, I let him control so much of my life, I lost myself." She turned to face him. "Before the night I came to your hotel in New York, I hadn't eaten dessert in a year. Ben didn't want me to gain any weight."

Alec's face hardened, holding back his anger. "You can eat whatever you want. Wear whatever you want. It's your life."

"I know." She wanted to seize back her freedom, but it was difficult to silence the voices of criticism. She had lived with the invisible chains for so long, she could hardly imagine a different life.

Deep inside, she *did* want to know what it was like for someone to truly care about her. But another part of her didn't know if that was ever possible.

Did she dare take the risk? Her heart pounded, but she forced herself to say the words. "There are many things I want. Some that I'll never have."

"What is it you want most of all?" he asked quietly.

She faltered, wondering if she dared to trust him. "I want to be free to make my own choices. Even if they're mistakes."

His hand tightened upon hers. "You are free now, Sarah. You can reach for whatever you want."

She swallowed hard and admitted, "And someday, I hope that I can be with someone who lets me be myself. Someone who will love me for who I am, not who he wants me to be."

Alec's gaze turned heated at the words. He leaned down, taking her face between his hands. For a moment, he didn't move, waiting for permission. She gave it when she stood on tiptoe and kissed him. His mouth was warm, inviting. A surge of longing spiraled within her, the desire to push back against all that she'd lost.

A reckless side of her knew that this wasn't wise, but she allowed herself to indulge in the forbidden moment. She drew her arms around his neck, and he pulled her closer. "Do you want to go back?" He murmured the words against her mouth, and she felt a surge of desire blooming within her.

She didn't know what she wanted. No, this wasn't a good idea. But her heart didn't believe it. Spending Christmas in his arms was exactly what she wanted right now. For so long, she'd been imprisoned, a woman caught up in invisible chains. She'd been told what to do and when to do it for so long, she needed to seize her freedom.

"All right," she murmured, though she wasn't at all certain it was a good idea.

It was growing colder outside. The wind was biting, and the streets were quiet with everything closed. He took her hand in his, and they walked in silence. Sarah didn't know what to say, but she wanted to believe that he was different from Ben. She didn't want to imagine that she could make the same mistake twice with two powerful men.

Alec might be playing with her emotions, using her somehow. And so, she decided to test him.

"Was it really a wrong number on your cell phone?"

It took an effort for Alec not to react to the question. If he told her that Carnell's wife had called, it would only lead to Sarah finding out about the business deal. And he wasn't stupid. The moment she learned of his connection with Ben would be the last time she spoke to him.

He didn't want to lose her, based on business dealings that had been in play before he'd even met her. He liked Sarah, and he didn't want her to get the wrong idea. But he was lying to her by omission. It was wrong at the deepest level, and that wasn't fair.

And so, he decided to reveal part of the truth. With a sigh, he admitted, "It wasn't a wrong number. I'm sorry for acting as if it was."

She waited for him to continue, and he added, "It wasn't Ben, either."

"Was it a woman?" she asked quietly. "Are you married? Or with someone?"

"No. I swear it." The thought caught him off balance, for he would never cheat on a woman. It wasn't something he would ever consider doing. He slowed his pace and looked her in the eye. "I'm not involved with any woman. Except, perhaps, you. That is, if you want to." He held her hand, stroking her knuckles.

"Why would anyone call you on Christmas morning?"

He didn't know how to answer that. She was right, that no business associates would call on such a day. All he could say was, "There are some developments that affect my hotel industry. Some of them are happening within the week."

They continued walking back to the hotel, but he could tell that Sarah remained unconvinced. He didn't blame her. "Do you want to watch another movie?" he offered, just before they stepped through the hotel doors.

"Not just now," she answered. "I think I'll call my brother and wish him a Merry Christmas."

"What about dinner? We could have a casual meal in the hotel dining room."

She nodded. "All right." But in her tone, he could tell that he'd planted the seeds of distrust. A heaviness caught him in the gut, for he didn't want to lie to her. But the truth would hurt far worse.

She was already withdrawing from him, distancing herself. Although part of him knew it was bound to happen, he didn't want her to go. If he wasn't honest with her—if he didn't tell her the truth, they had no chance at all to move past friendship. But what was he supposed to tell her? He walked past the front desk, and the clerk greeted him with a smile. She switched into English and held out an envelope. "For you, Monsieur Harrow."

"Merci." He tucked the letter into his coat pocket, not bothering to see who it was from. Instead, he was concerned about Sarah. When they reached the elevator, she pressed the button, hardly making eye contact with him. He sensed that the moment she reached her room, she would turn him away.

On a whim, he pressed the stop button on the elevator. Her expression froze, but this time she raised her gaze to his face. And he decided to throw caution to the wind and tell her the truth. He owed her that.

"It was Miranda Carnell who called."

Her face blanched, and her mouth tightened. "That was...not what I was expecting."

"Neither was I."

There wasn't fury in Sarah's expression—only a startled surprise. She paused a moment and said, "You could have told me the truth. Why would you hide that from me?"

"I didn't want you to think that I had anything to do with her phone call. I had never heard from her before today, and that's the truth."

"You lied to me only a few minutes ago." Her voice was brittle, holding back her emotions.

"I didn't reveal it right away because I knew it would hurt you. I don't know what she wants from me. I will call her back and ask."

She seemed to accept his answer and then looked him in the eye. "You don't need to shield me from the truth, Alec. If this concerns my life, I deserve to know."

"You're right. I'm sorry." But no matter how he framed the business deal, she would believe he'd betrayed her. It didn't matter what he said or did. She would think that the only reason he'd helped her was to gain leverage over Carnell.

In reality, he'd likely harmed the deal more than anything else. Ben mistakenly believed that Alec was sleeping with Sarah. Most likely the man would walk away from the contract. But even if the worst happened—if he lost the deal—he would still help Sarah again, without question.

He started the elevator again, feeling as if their friendship had slid onto shaky ground.

She stopped in front of her room and inserted the key card. "Just knock on my door when you're ready to get dinner." With that, she pulled the door shut behind her.

It was clear that she was displeased by his earlier secrecy. And she had reason to be suspicious. He should have told her the truth from the first, but he doubted she would understand or accept his dealings with Ben.

At the end of the hallway, Alec opened the door to his suite and remembered the envelope the front desk clerk had given him. Once inside, he let the door fall shut and took the envelope out of his inner coat pocket. The handwriting looked like his assistant's, and there was no name on the return address from Washington

D.C. Alec tore open the envelope. Inside was a yellow sticky note attached to a letter. It said:

This was sent to the office last week. Thought you might want to have it for Christmas.

– Lacey

The moment Alec started reading the letter, an icy chill flooded his veins. He forced himself to sit down, and his heartbeat raced.

It was a letter from his mother, dated from thirty years earlier. His lungs constricted, and his eyes blurred as he struggled to lock down his composure. At the time this letter was written, he would have been three years old. To see her words and this letter…a living piece of her…ripped the heartache open all over again.

Dear Alec,

I want you to know how very much I love you. If you ever read this note, you will learn things about me that you will wish you'd never known. But I want you to understand the truth.

About a year ago, I met someone and fell in love. I wanted to leave my husband and take you with me, but your father refused to let you go. I had no choice but to stay married to him, because I could not imagine turning my back on you.

I was faced with a terrible choice, one I never wanted to make. But I chose to give up the son I had with another man. I let him keep Carson because I knew he would be loved by his father.

Your father hates me for what I did, and he has that

right. But I made a mistake, and I paid the price for it. I hope you can forgive me and one day meet your half-brother.

If you received this letter, it means that I am already gone. Know that I will always love you, and you are my world.

Love,
Mama

For a long time, he simply stared at the note in disbelief. A part of him wanted to deny it, but how could he? It was her handwriting, though he didn't know if Carson had been the one to send the letter to his office. Was his half-brother trying to reach out to him? Or had someone else sent it to Lacey?

Alec had no memory of another pregnancy, so his brother must be close to his age. Since Eva had given the baby away, there was no reason for him to know about it. But Logan had known his wife was unfaithful. That was the reason for the sickening abuse. His father had been so consumed by it, he'd lost all sense of reason.

And now Alec had a half-brother somewhere. He flipped back to the envelope and studied the return address from Washington D.C. He didn't know anything about this man. But the letter had arrived on Christmas Day—a miraculous feat if there was one.

It was the gift of unexpected family. And he didn't know what to think of it.

Sarah hung up the phone with her brother, and she rested her head in her hands. Christopher hadn't been eager to talk with her at first, and when she dug deeper, she learned that he'd never received the money she'd tried to send him. She should have known Ben would find a way to cancel the check.

But even her apology wasn't enough to gain her brother's forgiveness. Their conversation had been strained, and she couldn't bring herself to confess the truth of her situation. It was humiliating to admit that she had been tricked into believing they were married. She'd made a fool of herself, and now she had nothing left.

Worst of all, her brother believed that she'd abandoned him when he'd needed her. Why would he help her now?

Sarah stood from the desk and walked to the window. It was late afternoon, but it was already growing dark. The Christmas lights gleamed in the distance, and she thought of Alec once again.

She'd known he was holding back the truth at first, and his withdrawal had cut her to the bone. Miranda Carnell had called him on Christmas morning, and he'd tried to shield her from the knowledge. She didn't know why; perhaps it was his overprotective nature. For some reason, Alec had suddenly changed his mind and revealed everything to her. She didn't know what to make of that. Was it guilt? Or had he decided to trust in her? All she knew was that Ben would never have done such a thing. He would have lied about it and never told her the truth.

Her head and her emotions were at war right now. She couldn't help but compare the two men. Both were wealthy and powerful, accustomed to getting their own way. But Alec cared in a way Ben didn't. She'd seen him staying up late, trying to find ways to keep the unprofitable hotels from closing. He didn't want his employees to lose their jobs just after Christmas. And his honesty meant a great deal to her.

He meant a great deal to her.

While she intended to go to Florida to see her brother, the thought of not seeing Alec again brought a sense of emptiness. He had given her so much, making her feel safe again. It felt as if her life was shifting directions, and now, it was time for her to stand up for herself. She needed to break free of the past to make decisions about her future.

The Christmas presents Alec had given her earlier lay upon the bed in the large, wrapped box. They were thoughtful gifts of friendship, and she appreciated them. But she honestly didn't know what else was happening between them. She couldn't deny her attraction to Alec, despite the warnings from her head. His kiss haunted her, making her wonder if she ought to give it a chance between them. He had never pushed for more, though he had revealed his interest. Her heart urged her to try.

But what if he used her the way Ben had? What if she let down her guard, only to face heartbreak? She warned herself not to get to close.

Sarah chose a midnight blue wrap dress and was considering which shoes to wear when Alec knocked on the door. A sudden rush of nerves caught her stomach as she opened the door. He wore a blue dress shirt and khaki trousers. His hair was damp from the shower, and his aftershave was a spicy fragrance with a hint of lemon. It made her want to lean in closer to his neck and breathe.

"I'm almost ready for dinner," she said. She just needed to put on her shoes and finish her makeup. "You can come in."

"You look amazing." He closed the door behind him, and the air was electric between them, an invisible magnetism drawing her closer.

Her cheeks flushed at his compliment, and she murmured her thanks while slipping her shoes on. It was a distraction she needed, for his very presence unraveled her good sense. She couldn't deny that she wanted Alec, and not only because he had helped her escape Ben. He was gorgeous and strong with a kiss that took her inhibitions apart. And though she was afraid of an uncertain future, the attraction between them seemed to only grow stronger.

"Are you still angry with me?" he asked, leaning against the wall near the door.

"I was," she confessed. "You should have told me about Miranda when she called." She stepped into the bathroom and brushed powder over her cheeks.

He nodded. "You're right. I can only say that I was startled by the call, and I wanted to protect you."

His blue eyes fixed upon hers, and she felt a dangerous rush of warmth flooding through her. He took a step forward, then another, until he was standing behind her in the bathroom. "I don't like the fact that Ben is stalking you. Or that his wife called. You deserve to celebrate Christmas without those shadows in your life."

She agreed with him on that point and tried to nod. But right now, she was overwhelmed by the emotions rising within her. Anger towards Ben for the elaborate deception. Fear of an unknown future. And forbidden desire for a man she shouldn't want.

Sarah rested her hands on the counter, her heartbeat quickening. She closed her eyes, trying to steady herself.

"Are you all right?" he asked. She could feel his presence behind her, and the air grew charged between them.

"I'm trying to make a decision," she answered honestly. A thousand fears rose up—fear of rejection, fear of the consequences. Fear of getting hurt again. A part of her wanted to lose herself in forgetfulness, while another part wanted to silence her own needs.

"About what?" He reached out to take her hand, and his fingers laced with hers. For a moment, she couldn't look at him. His very presence took her senses apart.

"About you." Sarah turned to face him, wondering if he would see the uncertain emotions in her face. She took a breath and rested her hand upon his chest. He reached out and caressed her cheek.

His unspoken invitation was enough. She wanted to feel cared for, almost beloved, instead of being used by a man. For the past two years, she had sublimated her own needs, putting Ben first. Would it be so wrong to reach for something *she* wanted?

She knew better than to imagine that there was any future with a man like Alec. He lived like a gypsy, moving from one hotel to another. When she returned to New York, she might not see him again.

It was taking such a risk. And yet, she almost wanted to do something selfish—to lash back at Ben for all that he'd done to her. To seize a moment for herself.

She reached up to Alec, standing on tiptoe. He leaned down, his mouth a breath away from hers. His eyes flared with unspoken need, and she drew her palm along the edge of his jaw. There was no mistaking the raw desire in his eyes.

But he was giving her the choice.

"What did you decide?" His voice was rough, almost primal in tone.

Her skin was alive, prickled with goosebumps. She drew her fingers along his cheek slowly. Then she pulled him lower and kissed him.

Her lips were warm, and Alec kissed her back, sliding his fingers in her hair. Though he didn't know what thoughts were running through her mind, right now he didn't care. He lifted her to sit on the granite bathroom counter, which made it easier to kiss her. The heat between them rose hotter, as if he couldn't get enough of her. He claimed her mouth, his tongue slipping inside to tangle with hers. A slight moan broke free and she parted her knees. He slid his palms up her calves until he reached the hem of her dress.

He knew that she wanted him as much as he desired her, but he didn't want her to feel pressured into something she wasn't ready for. He drew back from her mouth and murmured, "If you need me to stop, I will."

"I don't know what I want." She wound her arms around his neck and met his gaze with her own. Her cheeks were flushed, and she whispered, "I know this isn't real. And I know it's too soon. All I want is to forget about everything else. I want to steal a moment where I'm not thinking about the past or the future. There's only now."

He understood her desires, but he also knew the weight of guilt. He was involved in business dealings with Carnell, and if she ever found out, she would be furious with him. He was a bastard for letting this happen between them.

But the moment she reached for him again, he lost himself in her embrace. There was something different about Sarah. She gave herself fully, with no hesitation. He wanted to push away the terrible memories that haunted her and replace them with a night of surrender.

"Do you want to go to dinner?" he murmured against her mouth as he slid his hand up her bare thigh.

"No. We can eat here." She kissed him back, and he decided that room service was a very good idea.

He lifted her from the counter and carried her into the bedroom. From the window, Christmas lights gleamed against the reflection of the Seine. Slowly, he lowered her to stand and took her hand. He led her to the sliding glass door and stood behind her so she could see.

"So beautiful," he said, while he moved her hair to the side and kissed her nape. She shivered at the touch, and he reached for the tie that held her dress closed. He rested his hands there for a moment, still giving her the choice.

There was no discussion of a future between them—but she had only asked for a night to forget. And this was something he could give.

Alec opened her dress, baring her black bra and underwear. He slid his hands down her waist, kissing her throat as he did. Goosebumps prickled across her skin, and he was mesmerized by the swell of her breasts cupped by the black satin. He gave in to the urge to slide his hands over her breasts, reaching to unfasten the band of her bra. She leaned back against him and murmured, "You're wearing too many clothes."

When she turned, his breath caught at the sight of her creamy skin and her bare breasts. It took an effort to control the surge of raw need that claimed him. He wanted to lift her in his arms and lay her back on the bed, pleasuring her until she cried out in release. But he wanted the moment to last.

Sarah reached for the buttons of his shirt, flicking them off one by one. He lifted away his undershirt until his chest was bare. When she slid her hands over his pectoral muscles, his body hardened with need. She was looking at him in a way that made his heartbeat quicken. There was yearning but also a hint of sadness. He lifted his hand to her bruised cheek and stroked it. "He never should have hit you. It won't happen again."

She shook her head. "No. Because I'm never going back to him."

Alec leaned in to kiss her cheek before capturing her mouth again. He was caught up in the moment, in the way she yielded to him. He reached for her breast and cupped it, caressing her nipple. She shuddered, and her fingers dug into his shoulders. He continued kissing her, all the while stroking her breasts.

She seemed shaken by his touch, and she closed her eyes as if overwhelmed by the sensations. He was beginning to wonder if any man had ever taken the time to please her. He wanted to discover her secret places, to make her cry out in fulfillment.

Alec guided her back to the bed and removed the rest of his clothing, leaving it on the floor. He took a condom from his wallet and tore open the foil, sliding it on. Then he laid her back on the bed and leaned to kiss her stomach. He trailed his mouth lower before he caught her panties and slid them down. She nearly came off the bed when he drew his hand between her legs. She was damp with need, and when he stroked her, she tried to reach for him.

"Not yet," he soothed. "Let me touch you first. I want to watch you come apart."

"I don't—" she started to say and then amended, "I meant, don't worry about me."

He rested his weight on his forearms and stole another kiss. Realization dawned within him, and he murmured, "I'm going to touch you until you can hardly take another breath. I want you to feel everything you've never felt before."

CHAPTER EIGHT

Sarah couldn't bring herself to speak. Already her body was trembling with need, and the feeling of his hard length nestled against her was a temptation she could not deny. But she didn't want to admit that Ben had been her only lover. Although he'd never hurt her, he'd accused her of taking too long to climax. After a time, she had simply pretended that she was experiencing an orgasm.

The truth was, she had often felt used by him. No matter how hard she tried to please him, it was never enough. She wouldn't please Alec, either. She had little doubt of that.

"It's all right," she whispered, reaching for his erection. He was velvet hard and thick, and she saw the way his face tightened as she stroked him. But instead of letting her guide him inside, he clasped her wrists and pinned her back.

"Not yet, Sarah." He kept his grip light, but he made no secret of his intentions. "I haven't finished yet. I want to learn every curve of your body."

"You don't have to," she started to say, but he cut her off with another kiss.

"Shh. Just lie back and enjoy this."

She didn't know if she could bear it, but there was no choice except to let him have his way. With that, his hot mouth covered her breast. She felt a spear of pleasure thrust within her, echoing between her legs. He caressed her other breast while he suckled the first, and she gripped the bedcovers.

His mouth moved to the second breast, and this time, he slid his finger against her cleft. God above, but she was stunned with her body's response. He was tantalizing her, drawing out the feelings. When he circled her clitoris with his thumb, a tremor began to form within her. She was aching, arching against him. His tongue worked at her nipple simultaneously, and she sobbed out a breath while she felt herself growing slicker. A primal rhythm caught her, and she pressed back against his fingers. He rewarded her by entering her moist depths with two fingers, stroking her from inside.

She bent her knees, waiting for him to enter her. Instead, he kept up the rhythm, guiding her closer and closer to the peak. She wanted so badly to let go, but her body refused to surrender. It was as if she were fighting against herself and the woman she used to be.

"I've never wanted any woman as much as I want you," he said against her ear. This time, he cupped her bottom and lowered his mouth between her legs. Never in her life had any man kissed her there, and she was enslaved by the torment of his wicked tongue. He found the place of her pleasure and this time, he used his mouth to drive her over the edge. She felt herself rising higher, an eruption of shimmering desire ripping through her as she came apart.

She arched hard, and as the shudder of release broke over her, he entered her body. The feeling of his slick invasion made her let out a keening cry, and he kept up a gentle thrust as she climaxed around him. She convulsed again as he entered and withdrew, and she clung to him, shaking as he took his own pleasure within her.

She lost herself in him, meeting him as he penetrated. For the first time in her life, she understood that *this* was lovemaking, not sex. He had been attentive to her needs, drawing out her release until she was desperate to make him feel the same. She wrapped her legs around his waist, running her hands down to his hips.

"Let me touch you," she said, but he only studied her face.

"Later," he promised. "Touching you gives me pleasure. And being inside you."

He withdrew, turning her to her stomach. He dragged her hips upward and entered her from behind. The new position allowed him to penetrate deeper, and she was shocked by the delicious sensation. He quickened his pace, gripping her waist as he plunged deep.

Sarah couldn't stop the moans that escaped her as they thrust together. He reached to cup her breasts as he rocked within her, and when he stroked her erect nipples, she squeezed his length inside.

"Do that again," he commanded, and she obeyed, gripping him as he slid inside and withdrew. "I could spend all night inside you. But I want you to come again. This time while I'm in you."

He slowed his pace and moved her to lie on her side. Though he was still embedded inside, he reached around to stroke her clitoris. She was flooded with the sensation of his thick length inside while he caressed her hooded flesh.

Without warning, another orgasm tore through her, and her nails dug into his leg. He didn't move while she rode out the storm, shaking against him.

She backed against him, and he continued to enter and withdraw until he tensed and at last found his own release. She lay in his arms, feeling satisfied and almost beloved. Her heart was still pounding, and she could hardly believe the feelings he'd evoked. Never in her life had she enjoyed such a night. She was cradled in his arms, his body still inside her when she whispered, "Merry Christmas, Alec."

There was nothing more satisfying than spending the night with Sarah. He had loved her twice more, and they had eaten a late dinner from room service. Although he'd barely gotten any sleep, he had no regrets.

He wanted Sarah to stay with him. In his mind, he envisioned a life where he shared his apartment with her, waking up beside her. This woman had ensnared him, and he wanted so much more from her.

But first, he had to ensure that Carnell could never hurt her again. This afternoon, he sequestered himself in the office to call Miranda Carnell. He didn't know what she wanted, but his instincts remained on alert. There was no reason to trust her.

When he dialed the number, her assistant answered, and he waited for her to call him back. In the meantime, he read through the budget, wondering if he could save the unprofitable hotels before they had to close.

The phone rang, and he answered, "Harrow."

"Mr. Harrow, can you talk freely?" came Miranda's voice.

"Yes. What is it you want?" He had no doubt Ben's wife had learned of the affair. But Alec fully intended to shield Sarah from the outcome. She was the innocent party in all of this and had only recently learned that her life had been built upon lies.

"I want you to tell me about *her*."

"No." He wouldn't even consider it. "Sarah was trying to escape from Ben. She knew nothing about you until a few days ago."

"Don't be ridiculous. How could she *not* know?" Beneath the contempt in Miranda's voice, he caught a trace of fear. "Ben and I have been married for ten years now."

He understood the woman's desire to assert herself, but not at Sarah's expense. "Leave her out of this. She left him and has no desire to return."

"Good." Miranda's voice turned cool. "I'm glad to hear it." He waited for her to continue, wondering if there was another reason why she had called.

She answered his unspoken proposition by saying, "I know that you and Ben have a business meeting in a few days."

He didn't deny it, and she said, "I want a virtual meeting with you beforehand. There are things we need to discuss."

"Such as?" He couldn't understand what Miranda could possibly want from him.

"You're going to need my help. He's setting you up, Alec." Her voice turned almost sultry. "I know the sort of man he is. And Ben has no intention of helping your business succeed. Especially since he knows you took her with you to Paris. I overheard him talking on the phone."

A coldness slipped through his veins at the invisible threat toward Sarah. He knew Miranda hadn't remained married to a predator like Ben without having her own defenses.

"Why would I trust you to help me?" he said. "You're more likely to blame Sarah for what happened when we both know it wasn't her fault."

"Ben enjoys the chase," she said. "He likes to make a woman feel as if no one compares to her. Until he wins her as a possession. Then he grows tired of her and discards her."

Miranda paused a moment. "I know what that's like. And you can't leave, no matter how you might want to. You belong to him, and Ben owns you, body and soul."

"He doesn't own Sarah," he responded. "Not anymore."

"Yes, he does. She just doesn't recognize it yet." With that, Miranda finished by saying, "Call me when you get back to New York, just before your meeting. I can help you gain the advantage over Ben. And in return, you'll help me."

Sarah didn't miss the strain on Alec's face or the tension in his body after he returned to the room. He sat on the foot of the bed, and she moved behind him, massaging his shoulders. "What did Miranda say to you?"

"She warned me about Ben. She said that he would try to ruin my business, especially if you're involved with me."

She continued working at the knots in his neck and shoulders, though he didn't relax at all. "I'll be going to Florida soon," she said. "There's no reason to worry about me." Christopher was the only family she had left, and she wanted to heal the rift between them. She'd have to find her own place, but she wanted to be closer to him so they could work out their differences.

"I don't like the idea of you going alone. Ben might

try to follow you." Alec caught her hands and turned to face her. There was worry there, along with the invisible tension.

Although she appreciated his concern, she wasn't Alec's responsibility. They had spent a wonderful Christmas together, but her problems were her own.

"I'll be okay," she assured him. No matter what Ben said or did, she was starting to regain her footing. He had threatened her, but now, she was starting to realize what it felt like to have a life without him. She didn't hold the illusion that she had a real relationship with Alec—last night had been about reclaiming herself. It had been a beautiful moment, a gift she would cherish. She'd enjoyed spending the night in his arms, and she held no regrets.

He leaned over to kiss her. "I have to be back in New York in two days," he said. "Vacation has to come to an end, unfortunately." The regret in his voice echoed her own feelings of emptiness. But now, she needed to pull the pieces of her life together and take steps forward.

"Can you help me book a flight to Tampa?" she asked. "I can transfer from LaGuardia."

He seemed slightly taken aback, though he asked, "Don't you need to pack the rest of your belongings from Ben's apartment?"

She didn't know how to answer that. "Maybe later." Right now, it was easier to walk away from her home with Ben. He had bought nearly everything, and even her clothes evoked bad memories. "I think I'd rather leave it behind." Though she knew she needed to face her ex, she still didn't feel ready to confront him yet.

And really, did she have to confront him? In a way, it was liberating to know that she never had to see him again. Or if their paths did cross, she owed him nothing.

"I can book the flight, if that's what you want." Alec reached out to tuck a lock of hair behind one ear. She tried to guard her feelings, but his gesture of affection only deepened the realization that she would miss him.

"Or if you want to wait a few more days, you can stay at my place in New York," he finished. "This doesn't have to end so soon."

Though she wanted to say yes, another part of her held back. She was becoming too dependent on Alec, and she didn't want a knight in shining armor sweeping in to fix her mistakes. She wanted to gather her own courage, to be stronger for herself and for what was to come.

She caught his hand and held it. "If I stay with you, I won't want to go. And I need to start rebuilding my life."

His expression turned heated, and he drew her to lie down beside him, their feet tangled together. "I don't want you to go, either. Spend New Year's Eve with me. Or longer, if you want. There are plenty of jobs in New York."

She lost herself in his blue eyes. "It's too soon for a relationship, Alec. You know it, and so do I."

"I'm not asking for more than you can give." His hand moved to her cheek, and then he drew it lower to the small of her back. "Take it day by day. As long as you need."

Sarah felt her body rising to his call, and the memories of lovemaking only aroused her more. The heat of his palm made her insides go liquid, and all her resolutions crumbled in the wake of her feelings.

She wanted to spend more time with this man, and that was dangerous. She had to gather her senses. Alec was a good man, but she knew better than to let down her guard. Everything was happening so fast, she felt almost dizzy.

"I need to take it slowly," she said. "I trusted Ben, and he lied to me. I couldn't bear for that to happen again."

A strange expression crossed Alec's face, but he masked it. She wasn't certain what she had said, but it made her suspicious of the conversation he'd had with Miranda Carnell. There might have been more that he hadn't told her.

He squeezed her hand and stood from the bed. "There's something I want to show you. It's something that was sent to me yesterday."

Curious, she followed him to the desk where he handed her a letter. She read the handwritten note slowly. When she realized what it meant, she understood the trust Alec had placed in her by letting her read it. "You have a brother."

He nodded. And yet, there was no sense of joy. Instead, his face remained impassive, as if he wanted to shield all emotions. She read it again and then realized why he seemed uneasy. His mother's affair had caused his father's abuse. "How do you feel about this?"

He shook his head. "I don't know what to think. But a part of me wonders if my father would have beaten her if Eva hadn't cheated on him. I always knew Logan was a bastard for what he did. But now I know he had a reason to be angry." He let out a ragged sigh and ran a hand through his hair. "It still doesn't excuse what he did."

"No." She couldn't stop herself from putting her arms around his waist. For the first time, she saw a trace of vulnerability in Alec and she wanted to console him. "Will you try to find Carson?"

"I don't know. I need to investigate what happened. For all I know, this note could be a lie."

She hadn't thought of that, but then, a man as wealthy as Alec Harrow had reason to be wary. Too many might try to take advantage of him.

"I agree with you. But if you find that Carson *is* your brother, it sounds as if he wants a relationship with you. Why else would he send the letter?"

"And how did he get it to begin with?" Alec wondered aloud. He drew her into his arms. "I don't know what to think."

"Just find out what you can," she suggested.

He moved his hand up her back, resting his hand on her zipper. He kissed her, sliding his tongue inside her mouth as he moved the zipper downward. She understood his need to be close to her, and she wanted the same.

But more than that, she wanted to heal the loneliness. And as he pressed her back to the bed, she opened her arms, trying hard not to think about a future without him.

The last two days passed by quickly, but with each hour he spent at her side, Alec regretted his business meeting with Ben. It felt wrong on every level, and he was already taking steps to change it. The discussion with Miranda was critical.

He had also begun searching for information on his half-brother and had contacted a private investigator to learn more about Carson. They had traced the return address to a business law firm in D.C. His brother's full name was Carson Evan Kildare. A simple Internet search had revealed that Kildare's law practice was thriving, and it wasn't likely that the man needed money of his own. But why hadn't Carson sent a note of his own to accompany their mother's letter? Was he simply making Alec aware of his existence? Or was there another hidden intention?

After he finished a hot shower, he found Sarah poring over catalogues while seated at the desk in his suite. He'd told her earlier that he needed to update the furnishings in one of the Boston hotels, and she'd asked if she could help choose the chairs and tables. He saw no harm in it and had agreed. It appeared that she was making notes about what to order.

He kept the towel wrapped around his hips as he drew closer. "Did you find anything you wanted?" he asked, coming up behind her to rest his hands on her shoulders.

She turned and stood from the chair, and her gaze slid over him. "Maybe." Her smile turned wicked as she stared at him. Heat flared in his skin when she put her hands upon his waist. "I do see some things that interest me."

Alec slid his arm around her, and she rested her hands upon his damp chest. "There was a square laminate table that would work perfectly for the breakfast area." A droplet of water slid down from his neck, and she traced it with her finger.

Her touch ignited his own lust, and he leaned in to kiss her. "What else did you find interesting?"

She kissed him back, her hands moving through his hair. Against his lips, she murmured, "I also saw some ergonomic desk chairs."

A laugh caught in his throat. "How…fascinating."

"Lumbar support is quite useful," she said. Her hands moved up his spine, massaging his bare skin until every thought left his brain. He needed to touch this woman, to make love to her until they both lost themselves in pleasure.

He wanted her to stay with him. He knew she was planning to leave, and he didn't want that. For the first time in his life, he'd found someone he cared about. She fit into his life in a way he'd never expected, offering her suggestions on the hotels and ways to improve business. But more than that, there was the sense that she was the missing piece. Sarah's smile humbled him, and with every day at her side, he was falling hard for her. He would do everything in his power to convince her to stay.

"I think you should show me," he said, taking a seat on the chair and letting the towel fall open. "Will this chair have the right support?"

Her expression grew intent, and drew closer, watching him. She studied his body, her gaze memorizing every detail, and he grew rock hard at the anticipation. Sarah loosened her wrap dress and lifted it away, revealing a black bra and black lacy panties. He wanted nothing more than to push her back onto the bed, tearing off the undergarments until he was inside her, but he forced himself to let her be in command.

She had been abused and undermined for two years now, subjugated to another man's will. He wanted her to hold the power now, to do whatever she desired. Slowly, she drew closer, and he fought for control.

Her hands moved over his shoulders, and the simple caress was electric. He tried to reach up for another kiss, but she pulled back.

"Wait," she whispered. She went to the desk and withdrew a condom from the box he'd bought earlier. Then she tore open the foil and rolled it over his erection. The forbidden touch of her hands made him harden even more. More than anything, he wanted to be inside her, and the tension was killing him.

"Take what you want from me," he said darkly. "You're in charge."

She bit her lower lip, and then reached back to unfasten her bra and remove her underwear. When she stood naked before him, he admired her, noting the curves of her breasts and the pale pink nipples that he wanted to touch.

"Move forward in the chair," she ordered, and he obeyed. She stood between his legs and leaned down to hiss him. He showed her his fierce need, kissing her hard, while his tongue slid inside the way he wanted to be in her. A soft moan escaped her, and she pulled back, drawing his mouth to her breasts. He took one nipple in his mouth, savoring the taste as he pulled her to straddle his lap. Her fingers dug into the back of his head, but he suckled one and then the other, driving her wild. God, he needed her so badly. He pulled her closer, and when her cleft moved against his shaft, he nearly lost it.

Slow down, he warned himself. *This is about her.*

He regained control, using his mouth to show Sarah how much he desired her. He continued to kiss her breasts, gently swirling his tongue against her erect bud. She was breathing harder now, pressing herself against him intimately. He gripped her hips, and she rubbed herself against him in rhythm. He wanted nothing more than to thrust deep within her, but he forced himself to let her take the lead. She was getting close to the edge, her face strained as she reached for her release.

When the orgasm struck her, she shuddered against him, her fingers digging into his shoulders. He could feel her wetness against his length, and she stood, helping to guide him inside her.

While he sat on the office chair, she began to lower herself, thrusting gently. He gripped her hips, helping her ride him, and she squeezed his length within her depths. She kept the pace slow at first, and the feeling of her wetness surrounding him, taking him deeper, brought his need to a razor edge.

"Are you all right?" she murmured.

"You're killing me," he gritted out. "But I would take this death a thousand times."

She smiled, claiming his mouth in another kiss. He held her waist, trying to encourage her to move faster, and when she did, the pleasure seized him with a force that overwhelmed him.

"Stay with me, Sarah," he said. "This doesn't have to end."

Her face was racked with her own rising need, but she lifted and lowered herself upon his shaft, quickening the pace. He was fighting to keep his control, but with every thrust, she drove him closer to his own release.

"I just want to enjoy this time together and live in the moment," she said. "Don't ask me for more."

"We're good together, Sarah. We both know it." This

time, he stood up from the chair, still embedded deep inside. Her legs wrapped around his waist as he carried her to the bed and lowered her down.

"We are good together," she agreed. "But it's too soon to ask me for more. Just…let it be." Her eyes grew hooded, and her gaze turned hot. "And I want you to make love to me now, the way you want to. Don't hold back."

He kept her hips elevated and penetrated her deeply. She gasped as he increased the rhythm. She met his thrusts, arching her back as they came together. He continued to move inside her, hoping she would consider staying with him.

He wanted her to give them a chance, to be together a little longer. And so, he slowed his pace, lacing his hands with hers. The tenderness nearly undid her, and her reaction shifted to yearning. "Please, Alec."

He could feel her frustration rising, and he withdrew with such slowness, she began to tremble. He made love to her slowly, drawing out her pleasure until she gripped his shoulders and gasped. The moment she came apart, she squeezed him hard, urging him faster. He obeyed, and claimed her, thrusting until he found his own release.

But the physical release was only temporary. For a time, they lay entwined in one another, and he kissed her, savoring the feeling of her body beneath his. It still bothered him that she would not consider returning to New York with him. And though he wanted her to stay, he knew how important it was for her to make her own choices.

His cell phone rang, and he debated letting it ring. At first, he let it go to voice mail, but then it began ringing again.

"You'd better see what it is," she told him.

Alec answered the phone, and his front desk manager informed him that there was a problem with one of the guests. The last thing he wanted right now was to leave Sarah, but he'd given his general manager the day off.

"I need to handle a situation downstairs," he said. "I'll call you, and then we can go out to dinner."

She rolled to her side while he got dressed, and an unfamiliar emotion gripped his gut. He didn't want to leave her at all. But he forced himself to go, knowing she would be there on his return. And he hoped that somehow, he could convince her to stay with him in New York.

Nearly half an hour passed before the room phone rang. Sarah reached over and picked it up, wondering what Alec had planned for their dinner.

"Hello?" she said.

"Isn't this interesting?" Ben said. "I called to discuss changing my meeting with Alec Harrow, and I hear you instead, Sarah. Now why would you be in his room?"

Ice flooded through her veins, and she nearly hung up before he added, "Of course, I already knew about it. My

PI found you within a day. It wasn't hard to figure out you were in Paris with *him*."

She took a moment to calm herself. He couldn't hurt her anymore. Since they had never been married, he held no power.

Quietly, she said, "I'll tell Alec you called."

Ben expelled a soft laugh. "Harrow hasn't told about our business deal, has he? He's been using you all along, trying to gain the upper hand over me."

Their business deal? What was he talking about? She guessed that Ben was only trying to feed her more lies. She couldn't trust a word he said.

But what if it were true? Was it possible that Alec could have hidden this from her? It would explain why he had stayed close to her. She had revealed a lot about Ben, information that Alec could use against him. But once again, she forced herself to remain calm.

"What do you mean?" Her voice revealed none of her rising anxiety, but she sat up on the bed. If nothing else, she would get as much information from him as possible.

"Six months ago, we began talks for a contract between our two companies. Alec wanted me to use Harrow Suites exclusively for Venture's travel needs. He was willing to give us a discount if we contracted with his hotel chain."

It felt as if the floor had dropped out from beneath her. No, it wasn't possible. She hadn't seen any evidence at all that Alec would do business with a man like Ben.

To the contrary—he had done everything possible to help her escape him.

"I don't believe you."

"Believe what you like, but we have a meeting in New York in three days," Ben said. "Call his assistant, and she'll tell you."

She wanted to deny it, but her mouth had gone dry and it didn't seem possible to form words. For a moment, she debated mentioning Ben's wife, but instinct warned her not to say anything.

And yet, if Alec *had* kept his business dealings with Ben a secret, how could she trust him anymore? Her mind was spinning off into confusion, trying to separate the truth from lies.

There was no way she could trust Ben or anything he was saying. It was possible that he'd invented the entire story—just as he'd deceived her in the marriage. Sarah managed to gather her courage and blurt out, "Every word you've ever said to me was a lie. Especially our marriage."

He laughed softly. "Does it matter? I took care of you the way I would have cared for a wife. You had money. A beautiful home. Everything you could have ever wanted."

"Why would you do something like that? You were already married." She couldn't understand why a wealthy man would go to such lengths, making her believe the lie.

He laughed. "The same reason any man has an affair.

Because I wanted you and because it was exciting. And you were so young and innocent, you thought it was all real."

"I was never enough, was I?"

He gave a soft laugh. "You couldn't possibly survive in my social circles, Sarah. You still can't."

A dark spiral of anger strengthened her, pulling her out of her fear. "I thought you loved me."

"No, I enjoyed watching you try to transform yourself to please me," he admitted. "I knew you'd find out eventually. I just didn't care."

The hurt within her transformed into a ball of rage. It was about power and control. To him, the false marriage had been a game, spinning a web of lies to see how far he could go. She despised this man and everything he stood for. And one way or another, she would be rid of him.

"I suppose you believe the lies Harrow is telling you. He probably wanted you to return to New York with him and start over, is that it?"

"Go to hell." She wanted no part of him, and the anger was making her stronger. "I may have been a fool when I thought I was married to you," she said, "but I have my eyes open now."

"You made a mistake in leaving me, Sarah." His tone grew softer, as if he were trying to sweet talk her. "But I'll forgive you. We were good together, and I know you miss what we had. I gave you everything, and I want you to come home."

It took an effort to keep her mouth from dropping open. How could he switch tactics so quickly? Did he think she would fall for his lies again?

"You hit me," she reminded him. "Why would I want to come back to you?"

"Now you're being melodramatic," he said with a sigh. "It was just a light tap to get your attention. I didn't really hurt you, Sarah. You know I would never do that."

"There's a black bruise on my cheek that says otherwise."

"But that was *your* fault. You made me so angry at the thought of you leaving, I lost my temper. If you hadn't tried to leave, I never would have done it."

She could hardly believe what she was hearing. He was delusional if he thought he could blame the bruise on her. "I have nothing more to say to you," she told him. "Just let me go. Don't call me anymore."

"You're overreacting and being too sensitive," he said. "Calm down and listen to reason." She was about to hang up on him when he added, "If I back out of this business deal, the details of our relationship will become public gossip. And if that happens, I will personally do whatever it takes to ruin Harrow Suites. Several of his hotel properties are struggling. He'll have to close the New York location, among others." With a slight pause, he added, "Or you could come home, and I'll forget about your…indiscretion. I'll sign the deal."

Her skin crawled at the thought. "No. I'm not coming back to you." She hung up the phone and tried to calm the troubled emotions inside her.

It felt as if she'd taken another blow to the face, and she sat down. For a time, she simply took a few deep breaths. She squeezed her arms, trying to gather control. *He's lying and is only trying to bring you back under his control. He doesn't want you. He only wants you to yield to his every whim.*

But her heart ached at the thought of being betrayed by Alec. She didn't want to believe that everything between them had been a lie.

And yet…what man would take a woman he barely knew to Paris? Why would he buy her clothes, a romantic dinner, and Christmas presents? Was he using her, trying to gain more information about Ben? Had she fallen prey to another man's sick idea of a joke? Her gut churned at the thought of it being a lie. She had given herself to Alec, believing it was a way of healing the broken pieces of her heart. Instead, it might be yet another terrible mistake she'd made.

Tears welled up in her eyes, with such fear that it could be true. Sarah clenched her fists and pushed back the emotions, trying to steel herself for the worst. Right now, she wouldn't draw conclusions until she'd talked with Alec. There was only one way to know for certain who was telling the truth.

She sat down in a chair to wait, reminding herself that Ben could be wrong. Alec might have been protecting her instead. She clung to the thought, praying it was true.

The sound of the room door opening caught her attention, and Alec came inside, looking sheepish. "Sorry about that. The front desk was having trouble with a guest who was hung over from a night of partying."

She nodded and then asked, "Could I borrow your phone a moment?"

Alec handed it over without hesitation and unlocked the security code. "Here. Or you can call anyone on the hotel phone if you need to."

The tightness in her stomach didn't ease, despite his willingness to give over the cell phone. Yet, he acted like a man with nothing to hide, which was a positive sign.

"I'd like you to call your assistant," she said. "There's something I need to ask her."

There was a slight furrow in his brow. The reaction deepened her uneasiness, but she forced herself to confront Alec. She needed to know the truth about whether he had any business dealings with Ben.

"What is this about, Sarah?"

The fear deepened, but she said, "Tell me her number."

This time, his expression tensed. "Not until you tell me what this is about. Something happened, and I deserve to know what it is." In that moment, she caught a glimpse of a ruthless businessman. There was no trace of sympathy or kindness.

A part of her withered at the sight of it. She knew. Deep in her bones, she knew that Ben had told her the truth. She met his gaze and confronted Alec. "You're having a business meeting with my ex, aren't you? It's in a few days."

His stony expression never changed. For a pause, he said nothing but continued to stare at her. She waited for him to lie about it, but instead he admitted, "Our meeting is on Tuesday, yes."

How could he? She forced herself to sit down on the bed. Her cheeks were burning with humiliation, and she felt as if Alec had stabbed her in the gut. Why had he kept this from her? Was it truly for his own gain?

"When did you set up the meeting?" she asked. "How long ago?"

"Before I met you."

Her feelings gathered up in a tight ball of physical pain. She could hardly find the right words to say. "I thought you wanted to help me. But you only used me, didn't you?" The sound of her voice came out hoarse, filled with all the emotions cracking apart. "You knew who I was from the very beginning."

His expression tightened. "I learned who you were on the second day. And you're wrong. I did want to help you."

"Because it would give you an advantage over Ben, is that right? Because I told you everything about him, and you could force him to accept your terms." His betrayal cut her so deeply, she could hardly keep back the tears.

"After what Ben did to you, I wasn't about to turn you over to him." His tone was sharp, filled with fury. He drew closer until he was no more than a hand away. "I could have told him where you were on that first day, but I didn't. I protected you."

Her eyes welled up, and a single tear escaped. She held her arms around her waist, trying to hold back the storm of emotions. Though she hated confrontation, she had to know why he'd continued this ruse. And if she started crying, she'd never get through it. With effort, she demanded, "Why didn't you tell me you had a business deal with him?"

"Because this is about more than me. I have a dozen hotels at risk, with more than five hundred jobs at stake. If I make the deal with Carnell, Venture will make all their travel arrangements through my hotel chain. It would keep those properties open and help hundreds of people and their families."

He reached out to take her hand, but she pulled it back. She didn't want him trying to soften what he'd done or distract her with hand holding.

His expression remained somber. "I still wanted to help you. Regardless of my business deal, I didn't want him to hurt you again. And he knows I was helping you. He threatened to end the deal because of it."

That *did* sound like something Ben would do. It seemed that both men were trying to manipulate each other for the sake of business. She stepped back, uncertain of what to say. "You should have told me.

Especially after the time we spent together." Her cheeks were burning at the thought of the intimacy between them, and her heart ached at the memory. Just like before, a wealthy man had taken advantage of her, and she'd let it happen, believing in fairytales.

"I knew you'd be angry," he answered. "There was no good way to tell you."

"So, you decided to keep it from me." She reached for her key card, realizing that it was impossible to heal the shattered trust.

"If I had told you the truth from the beginning, you would have run from me. Just as you're doing now." He eyed her key card. Then he softened his tone. "I know you're angry with me. But how could I jeopardize the livelihood of so many people for the sake of one person? It's not just my life or yours. It's Jasmine's and Dawson's, and Cora's. I don't want to shut down the New York property and lay off hundreds of employees right after Christmas. And if signing a deal with Carnell will stop it from happening, then that's what I'll do."

"Were you ever going to tell me?" She needed to know the truth.

"Eventually." He paused a moment. "When I first met you, I was furious with Ben for what he'd done to you. It brought back memories of my father's abuse." He closed his eyes as if to push back the invisible pain.

"I don't need you to save me anymore," she told him. "I'm going to stay with my brother now. I'm going to get a job in Florida and put my life back together." She knew it was necessary. Right now, she needed to get away from her past and start again.

"And what will you do if Ben comes after you again? He won't give up."

A thread of fear wound itself around her heart, even though she knew Ben couldn't force her to return. "He's married to someone else. He'll let me go." Though even as she spoke the words, she didn't quite believe them.

"Will he? He's already spent money on a private investigator." Alec crossed his arms and regarded her. "He doesn't want you to be free of him. To him, you're like a lost puppy who needs to be brought home again. And if that happens, he'll try to punish you."

Her anger tightened at his words, but she said nothing—because he was right. Ben had the money to continue stalking her. He had the means to manipulate her emotions until she was living with terror at every moment. She had become a shell of a woman, cowering at his control until she had lost herself.

"You're right," she heard herself say. Ben had already tracked her this far, and he would consider it a game to continue stalking her. But how could she set herself free? The only real answer was to stand up to him. "Before I go to Florida, I'll have to confront him and make him let me go."

Alec was already shaking his head. "Not if he's going to hurt you. I'll be damned if I stand back and let that happen."

"I'm not your responsibility," she reminded him.

"This is my life and my problem. I don't need you trying to control me the way he did."

He went utterly still. Though Alec was nothing like Ben, she needed him to let her handle her own problems. If she let him step in and rescue her, it would be the same situation all over again.

"I'm not trying to control you," he said quietly. "I just want you to be safe. I care about you, Sarah. I want to help." He reached up to trace the fading bruise, and the warmth of his hand softened her anger. She had feelings for him too, even if they were complicated.

"I need to tell Ben in person that it's over. I need to face my own fears."

But Alec appeared doubtful. "You need a restraining order, not a conversation."

She suspected that was true, but she wasn't ready to involve the police. "I'll talk to him first. Likely at his office. He won't make a scene in front of his colleagues."

For a long moment, Alec studied her. "Then let me come with you."

"No. It's better if I do this alone." Even as she spoke the words, she felt her own heartache resonate throughout her body.

"I'm sorry I didn't tell you about our business deal." His voice was haggard and rough. "I should have. But I didn't know what would happen between us. I thought I could help you escape him and that would be the end of it."

He stared into her eyes, and in them, she saw the unspoken emotions. "I've never met anyone like you before, Sarah. And after we became friends, I found that I didn't want to let you go. I still don't." His expression grew raw, and she felt an ache deepen inside her. She longed to go back into Alec's arms to forget all that had happened in the past hour. But she couldn't simply let it go. He'd kept the truth from her, lying by omission.

"There can't be anything more between us if you can't be honest with me," she said. "No more secrets." He hesitated, and she sensed he was holding something back. "Was there anything else you wanted to tell me? Anything else you've kept hidden?"

Again, the hesitation. But then he looked her squarely in the eye. "Ben cut off all your money. I loaned you ten thousand from my personal account."

Oh God. It felt as if the air to her lungs had been sucked away. "You weren't going to reveal that either, were you?"

He shrugged. "Not at first. But you said you wanted no more secrets. There are no more."

Her cheeks flushed with embarrassment. All this time, she'd believed that the money was hers by right— only to learn that she'd been destitute all along. She'd mistakenly thought that she was seizing her independence, but the truth was, she'd been borrowing from Alec. It felt as if she were falling into an endless pit, unable to grasp a handhold to pull herself out. She didn't want to be dependent on anyone else, and he needed to know that.

"Why would you let me believe it was mine?" she demanded. "Did it entertain you, having that power over me?" The sickening feeling inside her strengthened. She'd wanted to believe that Alec was different, but he was exactly the same.

"That wasn't my reason. You needed help, and I gave it to you."

"Ten thousand dollars was far too much," she insisted. "You shouldn't have done it."

But he appeared unrepentant. "I make donations to battered women's shelters all the time. This time, I simply donated to you."

That only made it worse, for she felt like a charity case. "I'm going to pay you back," she said quietly. "Every last penny."

He gave a single nod, but added, "There's no rush, Sarah."

After a pause, he asked, "I know this is a bad time to ask, but do you still want to go out to dinner?"

She had no idea how to answer that. After all she'd learned about his interference, her pride had taken a sharp blow. Her very survival had been dependent on Alec. And if she went to dinner with him again, she was afraid they would only end up back in bed again.

Right now, she needed distance to clear her head. She needed to gather up the remains of her courage and face her ex. Only then, could she consider a relationship with someone else. And right now, she doubted if she could ever be with Alec—not after the way he'd used her.

She met his gaze evenly and picked up her room key. "I think it would be better if we don't see each other again until your business dealings with Ben are over."

CHAPTER NINE

Alec was careful to give Sarah her space when he saw her at breakfast the next morning. She still maintained that she wanted to face Ben, though he didn't think it was a good idea. Given how much Carnell had done to her, the man would only try to humiliate her further. And he couldn't let that happen.

Guilt weighed upon him, though he didn't think he could have changed the outcome. If he'd told Sarah that he'd been involved with Carnell at the beginning, she would have fled the hotel after the first night. But now, she didn't trust him—and he couldn't blame her for that. He didn't deserve her trust. And though she hadn't truly broken it off with him, he could sense the distance widening between them.

Sarah emerged from the hallway, wheeling her suitcase behind her. She wore a green dress that accentuated her curves, and a black wool coat. Her blond hair hung loose around her shoulders, and she walked with purpose, as if he meant nothing to her anymore. He deserved that.

When she approached the front desk to check out, he waited for her by the door.

"The car is waiting," he told her, signaling for the bellman to take her suitcase. She followed him outside to the car. Freezing rain was falling, and he helped her inside the vehicle.

He offered nothing further and stared straight ahead while trying to decide what to say. The atmosphere was tense, and he wanted to reach for her hand to reassure her. But she was pressed up against the opposite door, looking outside the window as they drove to the airport. It was clear that she didn't want anything to do with him, and the last thing he wanted was to pressure her or make her feel uncomfortable.

And so, the silence continued.

His phone buzzed with a message from Lacey. *We found Carson. Do you want me to give him your number?*

A part of him wanted to say no. And yet, his mother had written him a letter, begging his forgiveness. He didn't know what he should do. And so, he revealed his phone to Sarah, and said, "Lacey just texted me about Carson. What do you think I should do?"

She eyed him for a moment, as if she couldn't believe he was asking her advice. But he needed some way of breaking the rigid silence between them.

She read the message and thought a moment. "If it were me, I would give him your phone number. You could talk to him and see what he's like. At least, for your mother's sake."

"I still wonder if he wants something. Why else would he send the letter with no note of his own?"

"*Did* he send you the letter?" she asked. "Or was it someone else?"

"He sent it to the New York office, and Lacey forwarded it to me here." But she had raised a good point. What if someone else had found the letter and sent it to his assistant? His father was in jail and had no access to his personal belongings, so it couldn't be Logan. "I don't see how it could be anyone else. But I suppose I can find out from Carson."

Her eyes softened upon him, and he was glad he'd asked her advice. He sent a quick text to Lacey, giving her permission to give his half-brother his cell phone number. Time would tell whether anything came of it.

"Where do you want to stay tonight?" he asked. "You're welcome to have your own room at my place. Or I can book you a room at the hotel." He didn't want her to feel obligated or threatened in any way.

"You don't need to worry about me," she said. "I'll take care of my own reservation."

"I do worry about you," he admitted. "I want you to be safe."

"You're under no obligation to me," she started to say, but he cut her off.

"No. This isn't about obligation. It's about the fact that I *care* about you. Even if you're angry with me, even if you want nothing more to do with me. I want you to be protected, no matter what."

She drew back from his anger, but he wouldn't apologize for his words. For a long time, she turned her attention back to the freezing rain spattering against the window. "Was any of it real between us, Alec? Especially since you had business plans with a man who tore my life apart."

He couldn't blame her for being suspicious. She had every right to be. But he had to choose his words carefully so she would understand his reasons. "At first, I only meant to protect you. But the more I got to know you, the more I liked you." He thought of the night she had baked him cookies and her generous heart. "You're beautiful, intelligent, and the kindest woman I've ever met. I enjoyed spending time with you, Sarah. And then when you spent Christmas Eve taking care of me, I realized I was falling hard."

He wanted to take her hand, touch her shoulder. Anything to make her see the truth. But he saw a tear slide down her cheek. If he touched her now, she might pull back again. And he didn't want her to feel threatened.

"I've made a lot of mistakes since the day I met you. I never meant to seem controlling or to take advantage." He laid himself bare, hoping she would understand. He now knew that it was better to step back, to give her the freedom she wanted. Only then could they build a real relationship. "But I want you to be happy, more than anything else. Even if it's without me."

The words pained him, but they were true. And he knew that, even if he let her go and gave her the freedom she needed, she still might never trust him again.

Sarah had no idea what to do now. Her mind felt scattered with everything she had left to do. She'd made an online reservation at another hotel, and she'd decided to postpone her Florida flight until after she'd spoken with Ben. The very thought made her stomach twist with nausea.

Throughout the flight, Alec had been attentive and kind, and he hadn't pressed her for more. But sometimes when she'd sneaked a glance at him, she had glimpsed yearning upon his face.

He lied to you, she reminded herself. *He doesn't deserve a second chance.*

She knew that…and yet, she couldn't deny that he'd made her feel wonderful. Even so, she couldn't take such a risk after he'd kept so many secrets from her. Their relationship had begun on uneven footing, and just like her first marriage, she'd fallen under his spell, believing in the fairytale. She had allowed the white knight to rescue her, but now it was time to rescue herself.

Although she didn't want to touch a cent of Alec's money, she knew better than to put herself in an unsafe situation. There was no harm in borrowing money until she found a job to support herself.

The old fears came back to haunt her, but she

reminded herself that she had to be a different woman now. She would be strong and face down the challenges—even her worst fears of all.

The car pulled to a stop in front of his apartment, and Alec waited for a moment. "Do you want to come up for a little while?"

It was dark outside, and she was physically exhausted from the traveling. A part of her longed to say yes, to sleep in a warm bed so close.

But she knew it was better to go to a hotel instead. "Not tonight. We'll talk more tomorrow, after your meeting."

He reached out and squeezed her hand. "Go to Harrow Suites, then. A room will be waiting for you."

She knew he meant the reserved suite he kept for himself, but she shook her head. "I've made my own reservation." He paused a moment, before he gave a nod. Then he closed the car door and stood on the sidewalk as she drove away. She could smell the spicy scent of his aftershave, and it lingered in the back seat after he was gone. It was a physical ache to be away from him, but she knew it was for the best.

She still had the cell phone he'd given her, and it made her think of Miranda Carnell. She suspected the woman was furious with her. Without even knowing it, Sarah had been the Other Woman. She closed her eyes, pushing back the shame. It was Ben's fault, not hers. Her only mistake was her naïveté, believing that what they'd had was real.

The car pulled to a stop in front of Harrow Suites, where she'd made a reservation. Though it probably wasn't a great idea, the familiarity of the place made her feel safe. The driver opened her door and brought her bags inside. She tipped him, and he drove away, leaving her to walk inside alone.

"Good evening, Ms. Walsh," Cora greeted her with a smile. The woman's blond hair was tucked back in a French twist, and there was genuine warmth in her demeanor. "I have your room ready now."

"He called you, didn't he?"

Cora didn't have to ask who she meant, but simply nodded. "Mr. Harrow told us you would be arriving soon."

"I actually have my own reservation already."

She started to reach for her purse, but Cora was already shaking her head. "You know he'll want you to stay in his suite."

Sarah thought about arguing, but decided it wasn't worth it. Instead, she simply thanked the young woman, who then arranged for a bellman to bring her bags upstairs.

"I know it's not my business," Cora said, "but he's a good man. The kind who would give you the shirt off his back to help." With a smile, she handed her the key cards.

Sarah started to walk toward the elevator, when she saw Jasmine wheeling a housekeeping cart down the hallway. It was late and well past working hours.

"Hey," she greeted the woman.

Jasmine turned, and a faint smile tipped her mouth. "Hey." She was wearing bright purple lipstick and her black and red curls had a sparkle of glitter on them.

"Did you have a nice Christmas?" Sarah asked.

Jasmine nodded. "Got my son some Legos and candy. He's spending New Year's with his dad. Thought I'd put in some overtime to pay those bills." Her gaze passed over Sarah. "Looks like you had a good vacation."

She felt the weight of Jasmine's silent accusation, but couldn't come up with anything except, "It was nice, yes." For a moment, she felt embarrassed, but then she added, "I want you to know how much I appreciated your help when I first came here. I won't ever forget it. I hope to repay the favor in the future, if I can."

Jasmine offered a faint smile. "We're strong women. We make our own future." And with that, she rolled the cart down the hall.

The next morning, Sarah pressed End on the phone to hang up. Although her conversation had been short, she felt as if she'd taken the first steps toward regaining her independence. Even so, she felt the desperate urge for comfort food. Cookies. Chocolate. Anything, really.

Because the worst was yet to come. She had also called Ben's secretary, pretending to be Alec's assistant. She had moved the time of his meeting with Alec to thirty minutes earlier. She intended to confront Ben in public and put an end to his stalking, once and for all.

But this time, she would be ready. She had ammunition of her own, and she wouldn't back down if he tried to threaten her again.

Her heart was filled with anxious energy mingled with hope. She flopped back in a chair, studying the bouquet of deep pink roses that had arrived this morning, along with a box of cookies. Alec had been careful not to pressure her, but he'd made no secret that he wanted to continue seeing her. She didn't know how to feel about it yet. On one hand, she was cautious, wondering about his intentions. But on the other, she recognized his interest.

A knock at her room door jolted her into awareness. She walked toward the peep hole, expecting to see Alec. Instead, it was a man she didn't recognize. He wore a name badge, and she suspected he might be a hotel employee from downstairs.

She didn't know who he was or why he was here, but she had no intention of opening the door. Her heart was racing like machine gun fire, and her breath caught in her throat. A moment later, an envelope slid beneath the door. It was addressed to her.

Sarah waited until the hallway was empty before she picked it up and opened it. Inside, she saw several graphs that made almost no sense. It looked like profits and losses for Venture—almost as if someone had insider information about the company. And from the look of it, Ben's financial investments were declining.

Who had sent these? She read through them for the next ten minutes, trying to decipher the information, when she suddenly heard another knock at the door. A moment later, the door opened. Sarah bit back a scream when she saw Alec standing inside the doorway.

"What are you doing? You scared me."

"Sorry," he said. "I really need to talk to you, and I was afraid you wouldn't let me in."

"You're lucky I didn't throw an ice bucket at your head," she said. "Why are you here?" It irritated her that he'd opened her door without waiting for her answer.

"I came to talk to you about my meeting with Ben." He remained near the door, and his expression was calm. "I want to know if you want me to call off the contract. I'll try to find another way to save the hotels and not deal with him anymore."

For a long moment, she kept silent, not knowing what to say. She hadn't expected him to make such an offer. No, she didn't want him engaged in business dealings with Ben, but she understood his reasons. If the hotel properties were struggling to turn a profit, it affected so many people's jobs and their livelihood. Once the contract was signed, Alec might not have to deal directly with Ben.

It wasn't fair to ask him to walk away—it would be a selfish move. And regardless of her anger at Ben, she could see no other way.

"I think you should try to save the hotels," she answered. "Do what you have to do."

And she would do the same. She didn't want Alec to know about her meeting with Ben, because he would only worry for her safety. There was no harm in confronting her ex at the New York office, because he wouldn't dare to cause a scene. This time, she intended to exert her own influence and fight back against what he'd done to her. For so long, she had remained in the shadows, afraid of Ben. But this time, she intended to confront him and ensure that he never contacted her again.

"Keep your meeting with Ben," she said. "At least hear what he has to say." She held out the papers to him. "By the way, someone slid these under the door a little while ago. They may be useful to you."

"Who was it?"

She shook her head and shrugged. "He was a hotel employee, probably delivering the envelope from downstairs. I didn't recognize the man, and I wasn't about to open the door."

"Good." He accepted the papers and returned them to the envelope. "I'll look at them later." Then he took her hands. "Are you all right? Is there anything you need?"

She wanted so badly to say, *Yes. I need you. I want things to go back to the way they were.* But she pushed back the words. If Alec truly had feelings for her, he would still be there for her, whether the deal went through or not. She needed to know if she could trust him.

And so, she shook her head. "No. There's nothing I need." She pulled her hands from his and took a step back. Her pulse quickened, and she tried to suppress the swell of emotions as she walked toward the window. "But thank you for arranging the hotel suite. I'm still planning to pay you for it."

Sarah heard his footsteps behind her. Outside, the window, snow blanketed the New York City streets. In a few days, the New Year's celebration would begin, and she wondered what changes January would bring.

She turned to face him and saw the hesitancy and doubt in his demeanor. It seemed like a lifetime ago that she had awakened in his arms.

"I want you to know, I would pull out of this deal if I could," he said. "I know Ben Carnell is only in it for himself."

She nodded. "And he'll cut down anyone who stands in his way." That was why she would use leverage of her own and find a way to help Alec. But if he knew about her plans, he might think she was undermining him.

He drew nearer to her. "I don't want to talk about Ben any longer." His palm moved to touch her back, and heat blazed through her. Despite everything, she was still attracted to Alec and longed to be in his arms.

But she was aware that if she allowed herself to be seduced again, it might end in heartache. She didn't know if Alec truly had feelings or whether he was using her.

A sickening suspicion dawned within her. She had just given him the financial data about Venture, and she didn't know what impact that would have. Had that been a mistake? She didn't know what to think, except that she no longer trusted herself or her instincts. When Alec took a step closer, she retreated again. "I'll see you tomorrow evening, and we'll see where things stand then."

She saw the flash of disappointment on his face once again, but he locked his gaze with hers. "I'm not giving up on us, Sarah. What we have is too good to let go."

While she wanted to believe him, she couldn't know for certain until tomorrow.

Alec tossed his keys on the kitchen counter while Marigold wove in between his legs. Though he didn't blame Sarah for her reticence, he hadn't expected to feel such emptiness. Everything made him think of her. The container of flour in the pantry reminded him of the night she had baked him cookies. He had enjoyed watching movies with her, sharing dinner, and talking late into the night.

And he missed the feeling of her silken skin beneath his, as he'd loved her. It was all he could do not to kiss her when he'd come to see her earlier.

He was exhausted from the travel, and he hadn't yet opened the envelope Sarah had given him. Alec took out the papers and read through the graphs and financial data. It seemed that Venture was struggling even more than Ben had let on, and Alec wondered how to use this information to his advantage. It was likely that Miranda Carnell had sent it, though he couldn't see why she would. Was she trying to warn him from entering a contract with Ben? He didn't see another way out, though he would prefer not to deal with the man.

He made coffee, planning to stay up late enough to decipher the data when his cell phone rang. The number was unfamiliar, but the Washington D.C. area code made him pause.

"Hello?" he answered.

"Your assistant gave me your number," a male voice said. "This is Carson Kildare."

A strange tightness caught in his stomach, and for a moment, Alec wasn't sure how to respond. At last, he said, "I received your letter. When did you find out about our mother?"

"Only last year, after my father died." Carson's voice held a heaviness, as if he had grieved the loss of the man. "All my life, he let me believe that my mother had died in childbirth. He loved her and always spoke of her with a smile, even though he married my stepmother."

"Eva didn't die in childbirth," Alec said quietly, unable to keep the resentment from his voice.

"No. Your father killed her." His brother's voice turned darker. "I never got the chance to know Eva. And from the sound of it, she should have left the bastard."

"I wish she had. She deserved better than my father," Alec admitted. "And I regret every day that I couldn't save her."

His brother grew silent for a moment before he said, "I didn't know if you'd want to know about me. I was the mistake that never should have happened. He killed her because of me."

"He *punished* her because of you," Alec corrected. "Every day for as long as I could remember. And I never understood why she stayed with him after I grew up and left the house. It was like she believed she deserved his treatment."

"Maybe she thought it was her penance," Carson suggested. "But I agree with you. She should have left." He cleared his throat. "I'd like to meet you, if you have time. Maybe after the New Year."

"She would have wanted that. I have pictures of her. Or some home videos you might want to see, if you can come up to New York City."

"I'd appreciate it." Carson cleared his throat. "And maybe some good can come out of all this. Now that you have my number, text me when you want to meet up, and I'll take the train into the city."

"Sounds good." Alec ended the call and poured himself a cup of coffee, feeling a stronger sense of hope. Never had he imagined that he would find family, much less a brother. His gaze fell upon the financial documents he'd received, and a sense of clarity struck hard. He knew what he had to do—not only about Carnell, but also how to compromise with Sarah.

He flipped through pictures on his phone and saw the Christmas Eve photo of her with the Paris lights behind her. Although the bruise was visible, there was a shining light in her eyes that caught his heart. He wanted to spend more time with her, to love her and make more memories.

But first, he had to make a call.

Sarah walked into Venture Enterprises, her nerves raw with anxiety. She didn't recognize the receptionist but greeted her, saying, "I'm here to see Ben Carnell."

"He's not available at the moment. Do you have an appointment, Ms…?" The young employee sent her a pained smile, as if she believed Sarah was here for romantic reasons. Oh God. She probably still believed Sarah was one of Ben's women.

She swallowed back her pride, reminding herself of her purpose. *Face Ben, tell him to leave you alone. Move on with your life.*

"Sarah Walsh," she answered. "Ben requested a meeting with Alec Harrow. I'm his assistant, and he'll be joining us soon."

At that, the receptionist's demeanor appeared confused. Then she seemed to shrug it off and answered, "Of course, Ms. Walsh. I'm sorry." She made a quick phone call and Sarah overheard her telling Ben's assistant that his 10:30 appointment was here.

She took the elevator upstairs, and her heartbeat quickened with each floor they passed. Today, she had worn black trousers and a royal blue cashmere sweater, along with a black pea coat. In her hands, she carried a leather folder, though there was only a notebook inside.

When the elevator doors opened, her stomach twisted, and a chill descended into her stomach. She walked toward the conference room, and Ben's assistant, Justine, was already rising from her desk, panic upon her face. Sarah had met the woman only once, but they hadn't spoken much. From the stares of his coworkers, it was clear that all of them knew who she was.

"Good morning," she said to Justine. "Please let Ben know I'm here. I'll await him in the conference room."

"But Ms. Walsh, he already has another appointment scheduled."

Sarah turned back to her. "*I* am that appointment. And this won't take long." Without another word, she strode into the conference room. The walls were made of glass, which made it easier for her own safety. She took a seat at one of the side chairs and waited. Undoubtedly, Justine would have called Ben already, alerting him to her presence.

When he entered the conference room, she almost stood from her chair, but stopped herself. There was a curious, smug expression on his face. His dark hair had traces of gray at the temples, but Ben was still an attractive man. She had always known he was older, but his confidence had attracted her. That, and his intensity. He'd known just how to flatter and seduce her, and he had reveled in the power.

"Sarah," he greeted her. "This is unexpected. If you'd like to come back in an hour, we could go to lunch and talk. I'm afraid I already have a scheduled appointment."

"I know. I was the one who called to reschedule it earlier. Alec Harrow will be arriving in half an hour." She gestured toward the chair across from her. "Please sit."

Instead, Ben chose the chair at the head of the table, making her feel subordinate. He waited for her to speak, and Sarah gathered up the shreds of her composure. "I will not be returning to the apartment. You can have whatever I left behind. But don't follow me again."

His expression remained neutral, and the silence felt damning. She waited for him to argue with her or to tell her that she was being unreasonable. Instead, he rested his hands on the table. "I'm sure you understand that I'll be turning down Alec Harrow's offer now."

She stiffened. "Why? Because I won't continue to be your mistress?"

He gave a nod and leaned back in his chair. "I am, however, open to negotiation. If you want to reconsider your offer."

She couldn't believe Ben was being so manipulative. Did he honestly believe she would ever come back to him? Especially in exchange for closing the business deal with Alec? Not a chance.

She stood from her chair and pushed it in, looking down on him. "Do not contact me. Do not have me followed. If you do, I'll file a police report on charges of stalking."

"Are you threatening me?" There was a trace of amusement in his expression.

"I came here so you would have no doubt that I'll never return to you." No longer was she a young woman, filled with innocent dreams of a fairytale life with a millionaire. Now, she knew the truth about what sort of man he was. And thanks to Alec, she had glimpsed a very different relationship, one where she was on equal footing.

Alec had been trapped in the position of having to choose between his business and helping her. But the difference was that he'd given her choices. He had never forced her into anything and had respected her wishes. Whereas Ben had dominated every decision, unless it was one he had made.

"Goodbye, Ben."

He stood from the table and blocked her way to the door. After a pause, he stepped aside to let her pass. "You were never good enough for me, Sarah."

"No," she answered. "I was far better. And if you don't sign that deal with Alec Harrow, I'll make sure every tabloid knows all about our fake marriage. I promise you that."

Sarah made her exit, but her hands were trembling. On her way out, she was afraid of running into Alec. She had no idea what to say to him. Ben might back out of the deal, leaving him with no means of saving those hotels.

And it would be her fault.

A sickening sense of fear caught her, even as she glanced back and watched Ben pull out his cell phone to make a call. She hurried past his assistant and punched the elevator door button.

It had felt good to lash back at Ben, to threaten him just as he'd done. Yet now, she realized that she had only made the situation worse. He was a man who enjoyed winning.

And if he cancelled the contract, hotel properties would close. Employees like Jasmine and Cora would lose their jobs.

The elevator doors closed, and Sarah leaned back against the side wall.

What had she done?

CHAPTER TEN

Alec was about to step into the elevator when Sarah emerged, her face stricken and white. He'd never expected to see her here, and from the shock of her expression, something bad had happened. He'd known that she'd wanted to face Ben, but he couldn't believe that she'd actually come here alone.

He let the elevator close without entering and guided her toward a quiet corner. "What is it? What did he do to you?"

Her misery only deepened. Then she closed her eyes and took a steadying breath. "I'm so sorry. This is all my fault."

"What happened?" He took her hands in his. Whatever it was, he didn't doubt that Carnell was to blame.

"I wanted to face Ben, to tell him not to bother me anymore. He wouldn't listen." She gripped his hands, and he felt the telltale tremble of her fingers. "And now he says he won't sign with Harrow Suites anymore. I was so angry, I told him I would tell the media about our false marriage if he didn't. But it was a mistake to threaten him. When he's angry, he's not rational."

Her hands were like ice, and he stayed with her, wanting her to feel safe. "It's all right, Sarah. Don't worry about the contract anymore."

"But all those jobs…the hotels…" Her voice trailed off, her eyes gleaming with tears.

"I know. But I'll find another way." He framed her face. "I'd rather walk away from a bad contract than sign a deal with Carnell." It was the truth. He no longer wanted to do business with him, and he doubted if the man would keep the terms they'd agreed upon— especially considering Carnell's own business failings.

"I'm so sorry. I thought I could force him to speak with me if I showed up before your meeting. I never meant to ruin your contract." She took a moment to gather her composure, and he continued holding her hands.

"It's all right. I'm still going to hear what he has to say. And there are a few things I need to say to him."

She gripped his hands as if gathering strength. "Be careful, and don't trust him."

He fully intended to heed that warning. But even beyond the business meeting, his greater concern was Sarah. No matter what happened today, he wanted her to understand that she meant more to him than the contract.

"Will you stay and wait for me to finish the meeting?"

Sarah didn't look enthused by the idea. "I'd rather go back to the hotel and wait for you there."

"Or you could meet me at my apartment afterwards," he suggested. "The cat has been missing you."

Her spirits lifted at the mention of Marigold. But then she took a deep breath. "Actually, I think I should join you at the meeting."

He wasn't about to put her through that again. "No, it's not necessary."

But she stopped him and said. "I made a mistake by going alone the first time. I thought I had to handle my problems by facing Ben and telling him what I thought of him. And I hurt you without meaning to." She linked her arm in his. "This time, I'll go with you, to support you. I won't say anything unless I have to." With a slight smile, she added, "Besides, it will make Ben uncomfortable."

At first, his instinct was to deny her request. He wanted to protect her from Carnell and financially end him. But in Sarah's eyes, he saw that she was trying to overcome her fears. She'd been trapped in a false marriage to a man who had imprisoned her for two years. Carnell had controlled her, never letting her make her own choices.

And if Alec tried to make the decision for her, not allowing her to come with him, he was no different.

This was about more than his contract. It was about giving Sarah the freedom to decide for herself what she wanted, to take back her own control.

"You don't have to go with me," he began. "But if it's what you really want, I won't stand in your way."

The brave smile on her face was radiant. "Thank you, Alec."

He kept his reservations to himself, not wanting to undermine her. "If you feel threatened, I can end the meeting at any time."

She squeezed his arm in silent thanks. They walked to the elevators, and when the doors closed behind them, she stood on tiptoe and kissed his cheek. He caressed her cheek before stealing a kiss on her lips. He hadn't been lying when he'd said that he had things he wanted to say to Ben Carnell. Namely that he should stay the hell out of Sarah's life. He now had leverage over the man, thanks to the financial reports sent over by Miranda's assistant.

When they reached the lobby, Ben's assistant hesitated at the sight of Sarah. But she said nothing and guided them into the conference room.

Carnell was already seated and waiting for him. The moment he saw Sarah, he appeared irritated. "Why are you here? You're not part of this meeting."

"Sarah asked to be present," Alec interrupted. "And I agreed to her request." He sat down across from the man and opened his briefcase. Sarah took a seat beside him, and she gave him a knowing smile.

Her prediction had been right. Though she hadn't spoken a word, her presence *was* having an impact on Carnell. He appeared impatient and stood from the table. "This meeting is a waste of our time. We both know I'm not going to do business with Harrow Suites anymore."

"You're right." Alec withdrew the envelope Miranda had delivered and opened it. "But that's not why I'm here." He kept his tone neutral and said, "I'm here to ensure that you never contact Sarah again. She's been through enough. If you continue to text her, call, or threaten her in any way, she'll call the police and file a report."

"You don't know what you're talking about," Ben said. "And if you want your hotel chain to stay in business, you'll stay out of my personal affairs."

Alec laid out the copies of the financial reports. "It's interesting how you've managed to maintain a double lifestyle, given how badly Venture is performing. Some of these numbers don't add up." He passed them across the table and saw Carnell's face redden with suppressed rage. "I could contact the SEC, and they could investigate whether there's been any fraud."

Ben remained silent for a time, but then he stood from the table. "This meeting is over." His eyes held a ruthlessness that chilled Alec. "When I've finished with you, Harrow Suites won't exist."

But Sarah interrupted. In a soft voice lined with steel, she said, "Ben, sit down."

"Don't tell me what to do," he said coolly. There was no emotion whatsoever in the man's face. It was as if he had distanced himself and had no trace of accountability.

Like a sociopath, he appeared willing to do anything to gain the upper hand.

The hairs stood up on the back of his neck. Something was off, though Alec couldn't tell what it was. It was as if Ben knew something.

"You're an intelligent man," she said. The compliment seemed to unsettle Carnell, and he turned to her. "And you know when to cut your losses. We both know you don't want me. You never did. I was an amusement to you, nothing more than a pet."

She steepled her fingers together. "But have you thought about what will happen if Miranda decides to divorce you? She'll get half of everything you own. Perhaps more since it involved adultery. And I will not hesitate to help her."

Alec resisted the urge to smile when Carnell's face turned purple with rage. Sarah stood from the conference table. "As I said before, you're an intelligent man. You know it's not worth it to contact me again. Otherwise, I'll give Miranda's lawyer enough ammunition in court to take you apart."

Although the man's face remained rigid, Alec saw the twinge of fear. Carnell had received Sarah's message loud and clear.

She exchanged a look with Alec. "I think we're done here."

He couldn't have been more proud. She had faced her worst enemy and come out on top. After two years of being Ben's victim, she had fought her own battle and won.

They departed the conference room, and when the elevator doors closed behind them, she sagged against him. "I can't believe I said that to him."

"You were amazing," he said. "And I do think he'll leave you alone. In another year, he'll convince himself it was his idea."

"But the contract," she sighed. "I just wish something could be done."

"I have another company that might be interested in an investment opportunity." Though it wouldn't bring in nearly the revenue of the failed Venture contract, it might help them stay afloat for a little longer. He would keep trying until he found a way to bring in higher profits.

They returned to the car, and Sarah leaned her head against his shoulder. "Thank you for letting me come with you to the meeting. It was easier to confront him when you were there."

He offered his hand to her. "I want to be there for you, Sarah. For as long as you want."

She turned to him, and her expression held vulnerability. "It will take me some time, Alec. I don't know if you'll have the patience to wait until I'm ready."

"You're worth waiting for, Sarah," he answered. He leaned closer and murmured against her mouth, "And we'll take it as slow as you need me to."

Three months later

Alec stood at the door to his office, behind the front desk in the New York hotel. From here, he could see Sarah supervising the new breakfast doughnut bar. Jasmine had changed jobs and now worked in food service. She wore an apron and was standing behind the bar, dipping the hot doughnuts in melted chocolate before dusting them with colored sprinkles. She handed the plate to a young boy, who appeared gleeful at the sugary breakfast treat. The next guest chose lemon frosting, while a third chose strawberry frosting.

Sarah had been right. Not only children were enjoying the doughnuts, but the adults were indulging in the specialty. It had become a hit among guests, and word had spread fast. They had made a slight adjustment in the room rate to cover costs, and a bakery a few doors down provided the hot, fresh doughnuts every morning.

He saw Sarah approaching the office and opened the door. She was carrying two small paper bags, and informed him, "Miranda sent the latest samples. I want your help in narrowing down the scent choices."

He closed the door behind him while Sarah spread out the bottles. Miranda Carnell had expanded her cosmetics business, and he had signed a contract with her to supply all the lotions, shampoos, and bath products for Harrow Suites. She'd given him a generous discount, and in return, he'd allowed her to open a cosmetics counter within the hotel gift shops.

"What do you think?" Sarah asked, unscrewing the lid on one of the shampoo samples. She held it to his nose, and he caught a scent that blended orange and ginger. It wasn't bad, but he was distracted by her nearness.

"I trust your choices," he answered, setting the bottle down. He drew his arm around her waist and leaned in to nuzzle her neck.

"Alec, don't tempt me," she said, inhaling sharply when he kissed a sensitive spot. "We have work to do."

"I have a suite upstairs," he reminded her. "And we could take an early lunch."

She laughed and brought his mouth to hers, kissing him deeply. He could never get enough of her, and he loved her brilliant, creative mind. She had brought fresh ideas to the hotel chain, and it had been her idea to reach out to Miranda.

In return for Sarah's evidence against Ben in her divorce case, Miranda had agreed to sign a contract with Harrow Suites for bath and cosmetic products. Alec had been uncertain about it, but Sarah had insisted she wanted to do everything in her power to save the hotels. The two women had formed a strong partnership against Ben, and both seemed satisfied with the results.

"I need to answer Miranda about these samples," she said. "She's placing the orders today." Her expression dimmed slightly, and she added, "Her court hearing date is today."

"Will you need to testify against Ben?"

"I don't think so. My written statement and the proof I gave to her lawyer should be enough." She wound her arms around his neck, and he drew her close. "Ben is already in enough trouble."

"You're a brave woman, Sarah. And I swear, I won't ever let him come near you again."

"I'm not opposed to that."

After everything Ben Carnell had done, Alec wished he could put the man behind bars. But he was confident that Sarah was finally safe—and that was most important. Over the past few months, she had regained her confidence, and he couldn't imagine a day without her.

Her mouth softened in a smile. "If you want, I could bring the samples up to your suite in a few hours."

"Or now." He saw no reason whatsoever to wait. "You did say that Miranda wanted the orders as soon as possible."

She laughed and touched her forehead to his. "It can wait, Alec. For a little while at least."

"I'm holding you to that promise," he murmured. But when he pulled back, a tightness caught him, a slight rise of nerves. "But before that, there's something I've been meaning to give you."

Her expression softened, and she waited. He opened his desk drawer and pulled out the deck of cards she'd given him for Christmas. When she saw the kittens on the front, her smile widened. "It really was a silly gift, wasn't it?"

"No. It meant a lot to me. Just as you do." His nerves started hammering worse, and God help him, he knew he was going to screw this up. "Open it."

She lifted the lid and took the top card. Beneath it was a hotel key card. Her face held confusion, but she said, "Was this what you wanted me to have?"

He nodded. "It's a symbol. Well, sort of. I wanted you to have the key to every hotel I own. You can go anywhere, whenever you want. If you want to go back to Paris, say the word. Or Rome. Or London."

Her fingers curved around the key card, and emotion welled up in her eyes. "Alec, there's only one place I want to be. And that's in your arms."

She embraced him, and he breathed in the scent of her hair. He couldn't believe how lucky he was to have a woman like her, and he savored the moment. "I love you, Sarah. I want you to stay with me."

When she pulled back, her cheeks were wet with tears. But through her smile, he saw the happiness there. "I love you, too, Alec. And I don't care where I stay, as long as we're together."

He kissed her softly, and she yielded to him, making him long for more. She picked up two of the bottles from the desk and held them up. Her face was flushed, but she teased, "Maybe we should try some of these samples right now. There's a shower gel and a lotion."

"My suite. Now." He couldn't put together a full sentence, and he didn't even care.

Sarah took him by the hand and led him out of the

office. As he followed her to the elevator, he glimpsed the falling snow outside. His life had been turned inside out since she had fled her former life and come into his. Sarah had breathed life into his sorry existence and taught him the meaning of love.

And it was the best Christmas gift he'd ever received.

If you enjoyed this book and want to be notified when Avery has a new book out, sign up for her newsletter at https://www.averychandler.com/contact.
If you enjoy historical romance, she also writes books under the pen name Michelle Willingham.

Would you like a sneak peek at Avery's next book, *Switched at Marriage,* coming in February 2021? Read on for an excerpt!

Excerpt from

SWITCHED AT MARRIAGE

CHAPTER ONE

I'm pregnant. And the baby isn't yours.

Prince Amadio of Lohenberg stared at the horizon from the balcony of his bedroom, the numbness sinking deeper inside him. Any other man would have been furious, raging at his fiancée for her infidelity. As for himself, he felt only emptiness and the familiar solitude closing in.

Camille had left him that fateful voice mail, shattering their engagement and telling him that she'd gone to Italy. She'd begged him not to tell her father why.

How had this happened? He dug his fingers into the balustrade, gathering command of his emotions and transforming them into rigid control. As the heir to the Lohenberg throne, he had to maintain a calm façade at all times. He couldn't afford to make a rash decision or allow his own feelings to rise to the surface—not when this arranged marriage had meant a truce between his country and the neighboring kingdom of Badenstein, a means of ending the uprisings along the border.

Her betrayal had cut deeply, making him wonder what he'd done wrong. He'd tried to be kind to Camille, even knowing that he wasn't her choice of husband. Truthfully, the marriage had been the King of Badenstein's demand, trying to control his daughter by forcing her into a union she hadn't wanted. Amadio had been prepared to make the best of it for the sake of peace. But he'd never imagined that the princess would go this far to avoid marriage.

No doubt his tiny country would make headlines because of a royal runaway bride. Camille had dragged both of them into a scandal that wasn't his. And what was he supposed to do now? He refused to play the part of the humiliated bridegroom, appearing weak in front of his people. No, he would demand that Badenstein relinquish all claims to the disputed territory. Then he'd send troops to guard the borders and end the attacks once and for all.

Outside, the sunlight drifted across the country he loved, with its green hills and vineyards. The silvery river was calm, unlike the storm brewing inside him. Tonight, he was hosting diplomats from countries throughout Europe. It was meant to be an engagement party, a celebration of the peace to come.

He couldn't possibly attend and pretend that all was well—and yet, he could hardly cancel it at such a late time. It would be a serious breach of etiquette to deny the guests dinner. Many of them were staying at the palace, and explanations were unavoidable. But how could he admit that his bride had run away?

His mobile phone rang, and Amadio stared at Camille's number, letting it ring several times until he finally let it go to voice mail. Right now, he didn't want to hear explanations about her behavior or reasons why she'd wanted someone else.

She had left him with a hell of a mess. As far as he knew, she hadn't told anyone else what had happened. Amadio was the only one who knew that there wouldn't be a wedding. A headache throbbed at his temples as he tried to think of what to do. Now, he had to find a way of keeping the media under control.

Behind him, the door opened, and he turned to see his Lord Chamberlain. "Your Highness." Johann Sichermann bowed low. "The necklace intended for your bride will be delivered to you later today. I inspected it earlier, and it's exquisite. I believe the princess will be quite pleased."

"I couldn't care less about a damned necklace," Amadio muttered. The only thing on his mind right now was how to break the news. But he trusted Sichermann above everyone else, and he needed advice. "There won't be a wedding. Camille called it off last night."

The Lord Chamberlain blanched. "I am so sorry to hear this, Your Highness. Is there…anything I can do?"

"Not unless you can find another princess from Badenstein for me to marry," he remarked drily. "There will be diplomats and dignitaries at the engagement party tonight. See to it that they enjoy their dinner and entertainment. I won't be attending."

The thought of their pity ground against his pride. Right now, his head was throbbing, and he had no desire to see anyone. It sounded quite appealing to spend the night with a bottle of whiskey and drink himself into oblivion.

The Lord Chamberlain turned thoughtful. "Forgive me, Your Highness. But there was…something unexpected that I encountered this morning. In regard to the necklace, I mean. Something that may be of use to you. Or in this case, *someone*."

"Just send it back," he ordered. He had no need of a diamond necklace anymore. "And tell King Heinrich that I want to meet with him first thing in the morning." Now that Camille had severed their arrangement, he intended to force the sovereign's hand and demand peace without a formal alliance.

"Of course, Your Highness." The Lord Chamberlain cleared his throat. "But, as I was saying, you really ought to meet with the jeweler's granddaughter. When she arrived in Lohenberg this morning at the airport, she caused quite a stir."

"What do you mean?" He had little patience for this.

"She looks exactly like Princess Camille. I mistakenly believed that she *was* the princess when I first saw her.

206

You can only imagine how the hotel staff reacted."

A stillness slid over his mood, for he was beginning to see what the Lord Chamberlain was implying. "They could not tell the difference?"

Johann shook his head. "No, Your Highness. They were convinced she was the Princess of Badenstein. At least, until she spoke." He winced. "Apparently she has been living in the United States all her life."

"Send her to me in a private audience," he ordered. "Let her believe it's about the necklace. And try not to let anyone else see her." Although the woman's appearance could be a strange coincidence, he needed to judge it for himself. If she looked similar enough to Camille, she might help to buy him more time. He could pass her off as the princess for a few days while he negotiated with King Heinrich, and that would avoid a tabloid storm—at least for now.

"I will send word to her, Your Highness."

A thought occurred to him, and he asked, "Has the Badenstein ambassador to Lohenberg arrived?"

"Not yet, Your Highness."

If he spoke with the ambassador privately, it would give them both a chance to discuss how to cancel the wedding without causing a publicity nightmare.

"When he arrives, I want to speak with him immediately."

Sichermann bowed again. "Yes, Your Highness. But sir, may I suggest that you might reconsider attending the party tonight?"

Amadio gritted his teeth. The future of his country was hanging by a single thread, and he had no desire to socialize or drink champagne.

But he understood the need for discretion—at least until he could speak with the king.

Genna Hamilton stared at the Lohenberg palace and tried to gather the last remnants of her courage. It wasn't there. Although she was only here to deliver a necklace, she couldn't push back the nerves mingled with excitement. Earlier today, she had met the Lord Chamberlain, and then he'd called the hotel an hour ago, asking her to bring the necklace to the palace. Truthfully, she'd been shocked by the invitation. She'd never expected the opportunity to meet the royal family.

They'd sent a private car for her, and as they drew closer to the palace, she drank in the scenery. Brick walls surrounding the gray stone palace stretched high, while an intricate wrought iron gate stretched across the road. Around the castle, she spied several towers with copper rooftops weathered green. Ivy stretched over the surface of one tower, and she took a moment to savor the beauty. But when the black sedan pulled to a stop in front of the doors, her stomach gave a lurch of uncertainty.

She had been summoned by the Prince of Lohenberg. A prince. Her heart was pounding, and she wondered again why her grandfather had sent her to deliver the necklace, instead of coming here himself. Whenever her grandfather had spoken of his homeland of Lohenberg, there'd been a wistfulness in his tone, but also the sense that he would never go back. Yet, he'd asked her to come in his place.

Genna had brought the bridal gift with her—a diamond necklace that was worth millions. A security guard sat beside her in the sedan, and the jewels were safely contained within a locked briefcase handcuffed to his wrist. She possessed the only key.

The driver opened the door, and she stepped outside into the sunlight, her heels wobbling against the gravel. Before she could take another step, she spied a door opening from the lower level. The Lord Chamberlain approached, dressed in an impeccable suit. Johann Sichermann was his name, she recalled.

"Miss Hamilton, it's good to see you again." His English had a trace of an accent, and he smiled. "If you'll just follow me." He didn't wait for an answer but led her toward the same doorway off to the side. A servant's entrance, she realized. Which made sense. She wasn't a guest here, really—only a delivery girl.

Even so, she was memorizing every inch of the gorgeous castle. How many rooms did it have? Fifty? One hundred? She hoped she would have the chance to see at least a few of the rooms before she returned to her hotel. Especially the library. She imagined a sliding ladder that stretched to the top of the bookshelves.

Mr. Sichermann led her inside and toward a narrow

marble staircase. Genna glimpsed large oil portraits hanging on the walls as she rounded one staircase and climbed another, with the security guard following behind them. When they reached the landing of the third floor, Mr. Sichermann saw her lingering gaze and remarked, "That is Prince Michael and his English bride, Princess Hannah. They ruled over Lohenberg for nearly fifty years." In the oil painting, the royal couple were seated beside one another, the prince gazing into his wife's eyes.

"They look very much in love," Genna said.

"They were." Johann cleared his throat. "But unfortunately, most royal marriages are alliances not based on personal feelings."

She understood the unspoken message about Prince Amadio's wedding and offered, "Sometimes love can come later."

The expression on his face was bemused, as if he didn't really believe that. "Sometimes." He paused a moment and said, "His Royal Highness, Prince Amadio, has asked to see you regarding a personal matter."

Was it possible for her heart to pound any faster? Genna tried to behave as if it didn't matter—as if she met princes all the time. "Of course. He will want to see the necklace."

"After he has spoken with you," he corrected. To the security guard, he said, "You will wait outside until the prince sends for you."

Genna wasn't certain what to think about that, but

there was no reason to argue since she had the key. "All right."

Mr. Sichermann continued down the hall until he reached a room with double doors. Three chairs were outside, and he motioned for the security guard to take a seat. Then he knocked at the door.

Genna heard a man's voice commanding them to enter, and her anxiety ratcheted up a notch. Was this a throne room of sorts? She imagined a large wooden chair and wondered if anyone else would be there. His fiancée, the Princess of Badenstein, perhaps?

She had no more time to wonder before Mr. Sichermann opened the doors and said, "Please go inside."

Genna hesitated but obeyed, expecting the older man to join her. Instead, she was startled when he closed the doors behind her, leaving her alone with Prince Amadio.

Oh my, was all she could think when she saw him for the first time. Although he was seated behind a large wooden desk, she could tell that the prince was quite tall. He wore a charcoal gray suit, and his black hair was combed back. His sun-warmed skin was a stark contrast against the white color of his shirt, and the top two buttons were open. He was a walking men's cologne advertisement.

A flush slid over her cheeks, for she hardly knew what she was supposed to do. Curtsy? Shake his hand? What should she say?

At last, she decided to introduce herself. "I'm Genna Hamilton." She stepped closer and offered her hand, but he remained seated at the desk and didn't take it. Awkwardly, she let her hand fall to her side.

"The jeweler's granddaughter," he said, and she nodded.

Even though he was behind a desk, power radiated from his demeanor. The prince stared at her as though he couldn't quite decide whether to toss her out or allow her to stay. His gaze remained fixed upon her face. Behind his blue eyes, she saw the flare of a response she didn't understand. Had she done something wrong?

"Would you like to see the necklace for the princess?" she ventured. "My security guard is holding it right outside. I'd be happy to answer any questions about it if you'd like."

His expression sharpened, and behind those ice-blue eyes, she sensed that there was definitely a problem.

This commission was critical, one she and her grandfather couldn't afford to lose. Not only because of the ten million dollars, but also because the princess would be photographed in the necklace. It was a once-in-a-lifetime chance to bring Seraphina Jewels into the international spotlight.

Her grandfather needed her help, and she intended to do everything possible to ensure that the Prince of Lohenberg was pleased with the necklace. He'd already paid for half the cost, but he could easily send it back if it wasn't what he wanted.

"Are you aware of your resemblance to Princess Camille?"

Genna almost flinched at the question. "Um…I don't really know." She didn't want to admit that she'd paid little attention to the wedding, much less the bride. She'd barely heard of Badenstein until a few months ago, since it was such a small country. She was embarrassed that she'd never bothered to look at photos of the prince and princess online. And it wasn't exactly polite to tell a prince that she'd paid no attention to his wedding—her entire focus had been upon designing the necklace.

But it wasn't entirely her fault that she'd ignored the outside world. Her grandfather had led a simple life in upstate New York, refusing to allow technology into his home. He had no computer, no internet, and sometimes she thought it was a wonder that he'd permitted electricity. Her only access to the web had been at school. Even the Seraphina website was run by a business partner, and it redirected buyers to their store in New York City. Genna had never been to the city, for that was her grandfather's domain. She was content to work in her studio at home.

Years ago, her friends had teased her about Grandfather's hermit ways, but the truth was, they'd enjoyed coming over to his house. They'd played board games, baked cupcakes, and there was a sense of stepping back in time. And really, she didn't think it mattered. Sometimes it was nice to wash the dishes by hand and just talk. Maybe that made her old-fashioned, but she didn't care. She designed jewelry, so why did it matter if she isolated herself from the world?

The prince stood from his desk and crossed to stand in front of her. His gaze was penetrating, as if he were pushing back every layer to find the woman beneath. "I need someone to stand in for the princess tonight. A great many dignitaries have traveled to celebrate my engagement, and Camille cannot attend the party."

She blinked at that. "I'm sorry, what?" Surely, she hadn't heard him right. Someone to stand in for the princess?

His presence unnerved her, for he was fixated upon her appearance. "You're going to pretend to be Camille tonight."

Well, that was blunt. And he hadn't exactly asked— he'd commanded her.

"No," she blurted out. "I can't do that." She knew nothing about how a princess was supposed to behave in public. And why would he ask her, a perfect stranger, to fill such an important role? It was impossible.

"Why don't you just tell everyone she isn't feeling well?" she suggested. "You can attend, and it won't matter if Princess Camille isn't there."

"I have my reasons," he said. "All you have to do is take her place. It's temporary." The hard expression on his face warned her that there was more to this than he was telling her. He wanted the outside world to believe that everything was normal. Why else would he go through such a ruse?

"Johann will show you everything you need to know. All you have to do is wear a gown, smile, and do not speak to anyone. If you remain by my side, no one will know the difference."

He was insane if he thought she could pull this off. "Absolutely not. I'm not going to pretend to be a princess. This is your engagement party, not Halloween." The very idea was horrifying. There was no reason why he should go through with such an elaborate façade.

Unless…something had gone wrong. Something ominous that he didn't want anyone to know about. What if something had happened to the princess?

"Has she gone missing?" Genna ventured. "Was she kidnapped?"

Prince Amadio's gaze had gone cold, and he ignored her question. "I don't want to alert the media. It's best if we go on as if all is well."

Then she was right. He wanted her to stand in, so that no one would know that Camille was gone. If they were quietly looking for the princess, it might be safer if the outside world believed she was still here.

Genna had vaguely heard that there had been fighting at the borders between Badenstein and Lohenberg. And if the princess had been kidnapped, it could mean an outbreak of war. "Then she's…missing?"

Another nod, but she sensed that there was something else he wasn't telling her. "I'm so sorry," Genna said quietly. "You must be so afraid for her. I hope she's found quickly."

His gaze swept over her, and he said, "There's not much time before the party this evening. You will have to look exactly like Camille. Johann will see to it that you have a stylist to help you with your hair and so forth."

"But—"

"When you attend the party tonight, we will claim that you're recovering from losing your voice. You will wear the necklace." He eyed her more intently, and she felt the scrutiny of his gaze. "It's a business opportunity for you."

She knew he was referring to the necklace, but this kind of opportunity wasn't what she'd been hoping for. The thought of being the center of attention terrified her. There were a hundred ways to screw it up.

"This isn't a good idea," she insisted. "I don't know anything about behaving like a princess. I still think you should tell everyone she's sick. It would be easier." She shook her head. "I'm sorry, but I can't do it."

The coldness on his face grew more calculating. "Then I'll send the necklace back with you."

The air seemed to leave her lungs. Although Prince Amadio had already paid half the commission, the majority of the money had paid for the diamonds. They needed this sale to keep the company afloat. But worse, if the prince refused the necklace, the outside world would believe that Seraphina jewels were not good enough. It could cause irreparable damage to her grandfather's business.

It was a power play—she could see it in his eyes. Prince Amadio was accustomed to getting what he wanted. And for some reason, he wanted her to make everyone believe that his engagement would continue as planned.

"What happened to the princess?" she asked quietly.

He ignored her question. "If you do as I ask, everyone will know that the necklace was made by Seraphina. You will be photographed in the jewels. That will be enough publicity in return for your cooperation."

His voice was resonant, but she didn't miss the subtle threat. It irritated her that he was trying to intimidate her for his own gain. And though she was inwardly quaking, she said, "Wire the remainder of the money to my grandfather, and I'll do it. But I'll only switch places for tonight."

He drew closer and she felt eclipsed by his broad frame. She inhaled the clean scent of his aftershave, and she suddenly wondered what it would be like to kiss such a man. His presence emanated power and domination. He was accustomed to getting whatever he wanted, and for some reason he wanted *her*. When he put his hands on her shoulders, her thoughts seemed to scatter like marbles rolling across the floor.

"One week," he countered. "You will pretend to be the princess, and if no one learns the truth about your identity, I'll wire the payment." He reached out to cup her nape. The heat of his touch made goosebumps break out over her skin. She imagined him pulling her closer, claiming her mouth with his. The vision was electric, though she knew it was only a royal fantasy.

"In addition, if you play the role well enough, I will reward you with another million dollars for your trouble."

Well enough? What did he mean by that? Color flooded her face, and she shook her head. "I won't sleep with you. I'm not that kind of woman."

There was a faint softening at his eyes. "That wasn't what I was asking. But you may need to pretend... affection you don't feel."

In other words, she might have to kiss him in public or hold his hand. It seemed almost incongruous that such a gorgeous man would pay her to do this. Just because she looked similar to a princess.

"What is your decision?" he demanded.

Six million dollars. For one week of pretense. It felt as if the air had been sucked out of her lungs, and Genna sat down. It was a dangerous game he was playing, and she didn't entirely understand why he didn't just tell the world that his princess was missing. She wanted to ask again, but something made her hold back.

"I will try it for tonight," she answered. "And I will decide afterwards, if I can handle it for the rest of the week."

Did you enjoy the excerpt?
"Switched at Marriage" will be available in print
beginning in February 2021 at Amazon and on the
author's website:
www.averychandler.com

It can also be downloaded from all e-book retailers.

Avery Chandler lives in Virginia with her children, her dog, and her two crazy cats. When she's not rescuing her youngest cat from climbing the walls, she enjoys writing more romances. Avery's favorite hobbies include baking desserts, completing jigsaw puzzles, playing the piano, and traveling around the world whenever possible. Visit her website at: www.averychandler.com. Avery also writes historical romance under the pen name Michelle Willingham.

Printed in Great Britain
by Amazon